A Taxi to Biarritz

A Pianist's Journey of a Lifetime

Mathieu Ortlieb

Translated by Y. Opsitch

RIVERSONG
BOOKS

An Imprint of Sulis International Press
Los Angeles | Dallas | London

With gracious permission from Éditions Hugo Stern (France), translated from the original work 'Baignade des Ours Blancs.'

Translated by Yann Opsitch.

ISBN (print): 978-1-958139-67-7
ISBN (eBook): 978-1-958139-68-4

Published by Riversong Books
An Imprint of Sulis International
Los Angeles | Dallas | London

www.sulisinternational.com

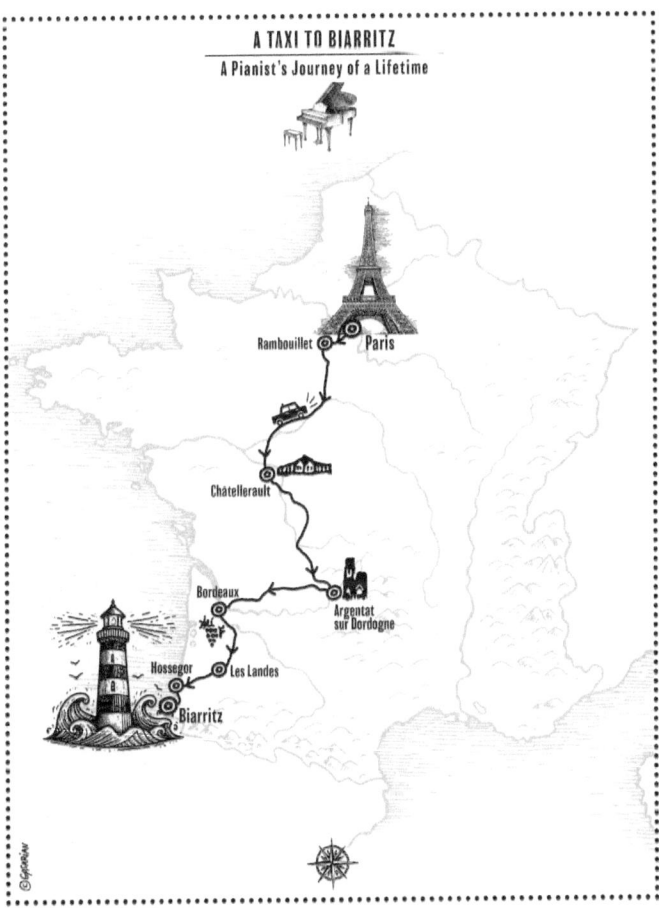

A TAXI TO BIARRITZ

A Pianist's Journey of a Lifetime

Rambouillet · Paris

Châtellerault

Bordeaux · Argentat sur Dordogne

Hossegor · Les Landes

Biarritz

They always say time changes things, but you actually have to change them yourself.

Andy Warhol
The Philosophy of Andy Warhol

To my life partner and my children.

*To my friend Carlo Scanduizzi and his wife
    Eulalie.*

*My gratitude to Isabelle Collin, Yann Opsitch,
    Irène Gasarian and Cyrille Blaise
    who kindly bolstered me during the writing
    of this novel.*

1

Yvonne hadn't slept a wink all night.

The day before, she had been reminded that she was about to turn 83, and although she didn't care about such an event, it had disturbed her sleep, reminding her of the cruel and ineluctable passage of time. So, with no hope of getting back to sleep, she got up at dawn. For some twenty years, she had lived alone in a 1930s millstone house at the top of a narrow, steep cobbled street not far from Paris. She lived there as if on an island with inaccessible shores. Her back bent from years of scales and *Czerny*[1] studies, she sat on a stool in front of the piano. Her eyes unfocused, she gazed at the walls of her living room, covered with old-fashioned wallpaper featuring flowers and foliage. It was all so dark, so boring, so sad... She couldn't help but grumble:

"It's ugly, it's ugly..."

Later, her gaze fell on a stack of sheet music piled up on the floor, tangible proof of her disinterest in the mu-

---

[1]*Czerny*, "Études de virtuosité pour piano," part of the obligatory repertoire for every pianist.

sic. *What a mistake for me to stop playing,* she thought. *Yes, what a mistake it was!*

Her eyes had moistened. There were no tears.

With slow steps, she made her way to the entrance hall and considered the door she hardly ever passed. It was autumn, and she suddenly thought of Toulouse-Lautrec's words: "Autumn is the spring of winter". For a long time, the painter's famous metaphor had entertained and even seduced her, but over the years, and perhaps due to her very old age, she now felt that the idea had lost its charm...

Soon it would be daybreak, and her shutters—the ultimate barrier she had erected to protect herself from the outside world—would remain closed.

She poured herself a cup of tea, nibbled on a rusk (no butter, no jam) and then, as she did every morning, sat down by her living-room window. Nothing much happened after that: the street was silent and deserted at this hour. As she mused on a *new past*, her reverie was interrupted by jerky footsteps: heels clacking on the pavement, amplified by the reverberation of the street. The noise drew closer, and when it finally reached her window, she recognized her neighbor's confident gait. One morning, she had caught this woman curled up in the arms of a man younger than herself and had immediately felt an emptiness. This image had awakened a terrible idea in her: that of her irremediable solitude. So, as if to ward off the *stolen kiss* she had just witnessed, she drew her curtains. Even now, she felt a mixture of contempt and jealousy for her neighbor.

She then noticed the mailman perched like a dancer on his bicycle, trudging up the street. Like every day, this was the signal: it was still dark, and she immediately put on a robe, walked across the vestibule, switched on the outside light, opened the door and stood in the entrance. Inconvenienced by the light, the mailman held out the mail. He squinted. She grunted a vague thank-you. In a foul mood, she closed the door without further politeness and placed her mail on top of the dresser. At that moment, startled by the high-pitched, trembling ring of her old phone, she jumped slightly and turned around. Staring at the phone, she said with a tone of reproach...

"No! There's no way I'm answering today."

Ever since she got up, she'd been obsessed by her past. A past that had haunted her for years. Yet she had tried to forget it.

She kept repeating to herself, *I've got to stop chewing on all this, I've got to stop thinking about it...* But throughout the whole morning, despite having repeated this injunction to herself a thousand times, she couldn't get away from it. She mechanically set about tidying up her cupboard that held linens, tablecloths and a dinner service she hadn't used in a long time.

Under a pile of linen, her fingers came across a cold object: a box... And she found herself caught up in the whirlwind of the past, the thought of which she'd been trying so hard to escape.

It was an old cake box—one of those lithographed tin boxes, almost always illustrated with pleasant country scenes—inside the box, she found a batch of old black-and-white photos with crenellated edges. Yvonne immediately plunged decades back into an unlikely period of her life. She held several yellowed photographs reminiscent of a concert: one photograph reminded her of the general atmosphere of that moment; another of showed several spectators... but who were these people? Yes, German soldiers, as well as a sparse audience, flanked by armed soldiers. Her gaze went from surprise to surprise... She raised her head and thought for a moment. But no, the event meant nothing to her.

Her hands searched through this strange past. Another photograph interrupted her musings. It showed a young girl with a frail appearance; her hands were resting on the keyboard of a Steinway, and she seemed to be playing... or maybe posing for the photograph? *But who was this pianist? And how did these photographs end up here in the first place?* She brought the yellowed picture closer to her eyes. Something was troubling her about this girl's posture, a decidedly curious picture...

Another photograph troubled her. It had a post-concert feel to it: the young girl was bowing and her arms clutching bunches of flowers; she was waving to the audience without looking at them. *No, no, it can't be. I must be mistaken...* she thought.

For what seemed a long time, she held the photograph between her hesitant fingers; she looked at the back and something was written. She turned the photograph over and over, deep in her thoughts, and read, "I played Schumann's sonata 1 in F sharp minor." She laid the picture down. A fear had seized her, and after hesitating to pick it back, her fingers grazed the photograph, and she read the following words, "First public audition, Bordeaux, June 6, 1940."

Yvonne was lost in her thoughts. She realized suddenly that she was humming the melody mechanically. She knew the score like the back of her hand, she'd played it so many times in her life... But *had she or not played this score in this theater, in Bordeaux, on June 6, 1940*? She had no clear recollection of the event, the place, the time or the audience. Nothing. Besides, it wasn't her writing; her writing was delicate, though dense and assertive; but this writing at the back of the photograph was devoid of grace; it was bland, angular, lacking smoothness. Oh, sure, the years had passed, and time had taken its toll. *No, no, I wasn't there! she muttered. The notched edge of the photo resisted her touch. But then, who could this young pianist be? She wandered through her memory, puzzled, vaguely worried. This photograph contained a secret—something inside her knew it—a mysterious piece at the core of a puzzle both fascinating and terrible.*

During her nap, she had a dream.

She was overwhelmed by a tohu-bohu of rales, various noises, children's voices, indistinct cries, distant screams... She could also hear the pounding of machine tools and the barking of dogs. A vision haunted her: she was walking through a moist, gloomy tunnel; in the distance far away, a slight flicker of light was trembling like a tiny drop of light resembling the flame of a dying candle.

The wall around her was viscous—a kind of thick, turbid substance resembling blackish blood, from which emanated a disgusting odor; she would remember later, without the slightest doubt, that, during her sleep, she had recognized this odor perfectly. She could no longer control her legs. She had felt as if she was rising into the air. Then her body gently tilted and floated horizontally above the ground. An extremely pleasant feeling of absence, but it didn't last. The width of the corridor started narrowing and when she tried to stand up again, her limbs refused to obey her; she was being tossed about in this rapidly shrinking corridor. Suddenly, two short words that she had once discovered—*Eng* and *Angst*—appeared before her eyes; two words that so aptly described the crushing of body and soul by reality. Flowing under her appeared a powerful river carrying a lot of debris swept up by a gust of wind; faces deformed by pain, floating among disparate objects but hurled towards her by what seemed like a reverse current. A powerful torrent had been hurled from the end of the tunnel, as if rising to attack. Suddenly, she found herself engulfed by a waterspout. She was drowning. Immersed all the way to the bottom, she swam blindly and desperately to get out of this hell. Breathless, she rose to the surface and found herself in the middle of a stormy sea, surrounded by giant waves several meters high...

She woke up, haggard, suffocating.

Her legs now hanging out of the bed, still shocked by the noxious atmosphere of her dream, she slowly came back to her senses. Playful chatter was coming from the entrance stairway to the house.

Children had settled down and were having fun, uttering enthusiastic and shrill little cries. At times, the chatter would come to an abrupt halt, the boys whispering to share a secret. Their seeming complicity had an air of adventure and mystery. Relieved by this cheerful murmur, Yvonne went to the entrance and leaned against the door so as not to lose any of their carefree chatter. Pained by her loss of interest in life—she had tried to end her own life on more than one occasion—she felt a compelling need to reconnect with the outside world.

After leaving her listening spot and taking refuge in the semi-darkness of the living room to chase away her evil demons, she set about cleaning up the place. Once she'd finished, as she liked to say, this *menial task*—a chore that she disdained and which she rarely did—she was surprised to feel a kind of well-being, a new sensation she'd never thought possible. Unless it was the prospect of living another day...That day, she felt an irrepressible desire to leave everything behind from her previous life. Then, in a state of mingled excitement and euphoria, she quickly washed herself, dressed simply, threw a few loose items into a suitcase and, without further thought, called for a cab to come and pick her up. Then, letting her mind rest and wander, she dreamed of a hypothetical future. Aware of the rumor of the street, she waited by the front door, patiently and somewhat calmed.

Yvonne was born on September 22, 1922. A few years later, as soon as she is old enough to listen to stories, her father comes every evening to read her a chapter from his favorite book: Adolf Hitler's *Mein Kampf*. Yvonne dreads this moment. She's afraid of her father. On the alert, she watches for the sound of his footsteps as they creak up the stairs to her bedroom. She hears these words [...] "*Men of the same blood must belong to the same Reich (state). The National Socialist movement must bring our people together to walk the road that will lead them from their present limited living space to the possession of new lands.*"

The young girl doesn't understand a single word of this National Socialist gibberish. Without her even noticing, Adolf Hitler's words sail from her father's mouth to her brain. She often falls asleep during the reading; as she sleeps, the words whirl around in her head, embedding themselves and creating confused thinking persisting over the course of the day.

One evening, Mary, her mother, dares to poke her head through the doorway. She looks sadly at her daughter, feeling that she has already lost her. Mary doesn't dare intervene and discreetly slips away like a shadow.

Yvonne would have preferred for her mother to tell her stories.

2

The driver double-parked beside the house. He glanced at the façade. He was a man in his forties. His face was impassive. He had long lived as if being absent from his own life, a life that had, as they say, failed to deliver on its promises; *but when had life ever promised anything?* he mused. Every day, he performed gestures without remembrance of the past, without a thought for the future.

He honked to signal his presence. His gaze wandered to the glove compartment; he took out a bottle of whisky, uncorked it and took a long sip, as if in slow motion. Then, he told himself immediately that he hadn't resisted the temptation to drink... *But what's the point?* he thought. He put the bottle back, glanced towards the house and got out of his car; he thought about standing there, next to the car, as if to mark his presence, but decided impatiently to ring the bell and stealthily sprayed his mouth with a breath freshener in an attempt to dissipate the smell of alcohol.

The door opened slowly, revealing a very old lady, certainly his customer; she wore a printed dress and had placed a hat with veil on her head. She looked as if she had stepped straight out of the 1930s. The driver, astonished by her attire, had to suppress a mocking glance and introduced himself. With a smile on his lips, he accompanied her to the cab, helped her settle in and fastened the seatbelt. As he did so, he noticed that she was glaring at him. Disturbed by this attitude, he gently closed the door, walked around the car and settled behind the wheel.

When he asked her where she was going, she didn't reply. He thought she must be a little deaf and raised his voice. She responded, saying, "Don't worry. I'll let you know the destination in due course..."

The tone and content of this statement disturbed him.

The light drizzle of the morning was giving way to a dense, persistent rain. Annoyed by the gloomy weather, Jean-Pierre—as the driver was called—started the car and noticed that his customer had forgotten to turn off the light. He pointed this out to her. However, she didn't think it necessary to reply. His features tense, he thought to himself that this was just going to be one more gloomy day—*Here comes another ruined day!*

Trying to put this thought out of his mind, he started the car. Having reached the top of the street, he turned right, came upon a deserted street poorly-lit, followed it for a while, then drove under the *Arcueil* tunnel and emerged, after a hundred meters, on the main belt road that surrounds Paris.

From time to time, he glanced at his passenger through his rearview mirror. When they reached *Avenue d'Ivry*, and coming close to the edge of a hundred-meter-long wall, Yvonne asked him to slow down. At her request, he parked in front of a large entrance gateway leading into a courtyard. At the entrance one could still read, although quite faded, the painted sign of an old factory named *Panhard-et-Levassor*. Gloomily, he watched the rain falling and already regretted not having canceled the ride.

The monotonous, back-and-forth squeaking of the windshield wiper didn't help his mood. He cast a furtive glance backwards: she was sitting in a hunched position, her face as drawn with sorrow. The head bobbling, she kept her eyes on the entrance of the *Panhard-et-Levassor* factory...Suddenly, she recalled the extraordinary chaos of sounds the deafening noise of a machine tool, a loud factory siren, the rumor of confused voices, one of which was shouting orders in German.

A door slammed; frightened, she felt the same fear she had once experienced and shrank to the bottom of her seat. Intuitively, Jean-Pierre turned around and saw her terrified expression.

"Are you all right, Madame?"

Startled, she realized it was the first time she'd ever been called Madame.

She gasped slightly. She had always been called Mademoiselle, as she was not known to have had any love affairs or romantic relationships of any kind. Even during her short career as a concert performer, about which she tended to be discreet throughout her life, she was never seen in the company of a man.

Yvonne answered at last; with restraint, she lowered and then raised her eyelids and made an almost imperceptible sign with her hand, more elusive than reassuring.

"Are you expecting someone?" asked the driver tactfully, as the slightest detail could set her off. He could feel it.

Still reeling from these reminiscences, she shook her head evasively. Yvonne's thoughts were so far away...

"So, can I drive?" he said, turning the ignition back on.

She suddenly graced him with a fleeting smile, and in a tone that seemed harmless, but was meant to be reassuring, she added:

"I'm not crazy, you know! I know what I'm doing, and I know exactly what I want."

He was perplexed by this statement, with its thousand undertones. He raised his eyebrows, twitched his mouth slightly, then drove off. When they reached the *Avenue de Choisy*, Yvonne, aware of the awkwardness being built up between them, stammered in a timid voice:

"May I know your name?"

"You mean, my first name?

"Yes, your first name ... "

"Jean-Pierre."

"Jean-Pierre, I'm terrible at remembering first names, I forget them almost immediately, pschitt! Just like that!

So don't blame me if I ask you again later. You know, memory plays tricks... Do you want to check if everything's okay with me? By the way, my first name is Yvonne."

It was still premature for her to ask him to call her Mademoiselle. Jean-Pierre met her gaze in the rearview mirror and gave her a courteous but reserved smile.

"Well, why don't you ask me where we are!" said Yvonne.

When he didn't answer, she tried to motivate him, saying,

"Ask me, for example, what town we're in."

He was a little taken aback and said, "What town are we in?"

She replied, "But that was only an example! Are you doing that on purpose?"

Smiling, Jean-Pierre nodded as if to agree. He furtively met her gaze. Yvonne's eyes said: *He thinks I'm crazy!*

"So, what day is it today?" Jean-Pierre continued, getting caught up in the game.

"Uh... Tuesday! It's Tuesday, isn't it?"

"Well, missed it, it's Wednesday!"

"Wednesday, Uh? I'm surprised. Are you sure? Oh well, after all, Monday, Tuesday, Friday, who cares," she replied with a casual wave of her hand and continuing, "In any case, the question doesn't weigh much in one's life, does it? If it were only a matter of forgetting... Let's just say it's more like negligence. But let me reassure you, I'm doing fine for my age! I'm often told I look younger. Don't you think I look younger?"

Jean-Pierre didn't take up the challenge. In truth, he couldn't care less about his client's age. She was a customer, and that was that. He drove his cab entering the *Place d'Italie* round about, but as she still didn't give him any instructions, he contented himself with following the flow of cars and turned around once, then a second time. Before a third attempt, he took the lead and asked,

"Madame, what do I do now? Where should I go?"

"Take this boulevard!" she said suddenly, annoyed at being called Madame and thinking *It's time I told him to call me Mademoiselle...*

About to attempt a particularly risky maneuver, Jean-Pierre tried to satisfy her, but she changed her mind:

"No! Take the next one, there, towards *Gare d'Austerlitz.*"

With great skillfulness, he corrected his trajectory and swerved into *Boulevard de l'Hôpital*. At that point, he realized that he had been deeply intrigued by this woman's behavior for some time—from the very beginning, in fact. Glancing back, he thought, *Strange mood swings, very strange indeed... The way she goes from being courteous, even complicit at times, to scowling in an almost hostile manner! But is she doing it on purpose?*

These musings only fed the doubts he entertained about his client's state of health.

He asked, "Do you need to catch a train?"

"A train? Yes, perhaps... I'm not sure... The truth is, I haven't decided anything yet. Right now, I just want to continue the ride..." She thought, *why does he keep asking me questions?*

"Continuing the ride is a bit vague, isn't it..." ventured the driver.

"But that is what I want, just to be driven around as I please. I want to take my time..."

Her reaction was so dry, so peremptory, so unkind, that he immediately felt like putting an end to the ride. He had enough to worry about without adding to it. But he pulled himself together, thinking *perhaps she has Alzheimer's?*

Definitely this is not my day, he thought.

Ever since he'd become a taxi driver, he'd always made a point of maintaining a minimum of rigor in all circumstances, such as keeping a certain distance from his customers, both literally and figuratively, and being completely honest with them. But now he was beginning to realize that these principles had their limits. So, he thought of a way to probe his client further, without rushing her:

"I didn't quite understand what you wanted... You're telling me that you want to take your time... All right. But what does that actually mean?"

"I'm not in a hurry..."

How should he take this answer, which wasn't an answer at all? Annoyed, Jean-Pierre frowned.

A little later, he stopped at a pedestrian crossing and noticed how she was glaring at passers-by. A young woman crossing the street met his gaze. Apparently frightened, she hurried on. When the light turned green, Yvonne spoke up:

"Doesn't it surprise you to see all these faces? And nothing in common between them," she added with an air of mystery. "And to think we'll never know any of these people..."

But Jean-Pierre wasn't listening. Was she going to continue to get on his nerves like this?

"All these people passing by," she continued after a short pause, "all these people with whom we might have had the opportunity to share things in life that we'll never share, for sure. Doesn't it have the same effect on you? It disturbs me terribly to think about this..."

Then, as if her speech had suddenly evaporated, she stopped speaking. For the next few minutes, Jean-Pierre tried to think about the question she had raised, but it didn't really inspire him; his mind wasn't in itin fact, he wasn't thinking about anything. He was still feeling the grip of a recent tragedy. He had become a gambling addict and in the space of a few months had squandered all his savings. His wife had left him, and that was the only thing on his mind today. So, philosophizing and gossiping about anything and everything wasn't really on the agenda.

After a while, Yvonne's voice once again could be heard:

"I remember a poet who said: *Every encounter dislocates and reconstructs us.*[2]

What do you think?"

What do I think? Mused Jean-Pierre.

In his cultural exiguity, reluctant to debate philosophy or poetry, he let out a big sigh. In truth, he didn't think anything of it. For years, he'd seen little point even of thinking. So, he simply replied with a touch of cynicism that, as far as his experience was concerned, encounters had rather dislocated him altogether...

Disappointed that he was showing so little interest in the discussion, Mademoiselle withdrew into herself, and coldly asked him to drive to *Gare d'Austerlitz*. Then she retreated into silence. Of course, Jean-Pierre blamed himself for having spoiled the beginning of a dialogue, but could it have been otherwise? From that moment on, he made a firm commitment to himself that he would just do his job, nothing else.

---

[2]*Hugo Von Hoffmansthal*, Austrian poet of the 19th century and one of the founders of the Salzburg Festival.

3

The cab entered the departure area of the train station *Gare d'Austerlitz* and parked in a drop-off zone. Yvonne was not moving. The driver cocked his head back to see what his client was planning to do. *Did she not want to catch a train? If not, why had she asked him to pull over?* For her part, Yvonne was remembering the photos she had discovered that very morning. One by one, the images came back to her: the concert … Bordeaux … This young girl, this young pianist … Jewish … Despite her efforts, Yvonne still couldn't put a name to that beautiful face ….

She was watching the incessant comings and goings of passers-by on their way to the train platforms. Suddenly, she was caught up in what resembled hallucinations, with sights and sounds from a distant past: fifty Jews flanked by French policemen; a yellow star sewn on the left side of their chests, these deportees were walking with their heads down, in close ranks. She could see travelers coming and going with indifference, bypassing what looked like a funeral procession, while others expressed a sort of disgust as they passed. A young girl—she must have been barely seventeen—suddenly broke away from the procession, threw herself against the cab and literally glued her face to the rear window. She seemed desperate to speak to Yvonne. Her lips were moving, but not a sound could be heard; no doubt she was calling for help, for her face expressed extraordinary terror. Yvonne was spellbound. No, it couldn't be her! That face, disfigured by silent screams, that face she now recognized was her friend Myriam! Yes, it was her, there was no doubt about it! How could she have forgotten?

Yvonne had met Myriam a few years before at the music conservatory. They had quickly become accomplices, then inseparable friends. It was she who had reassured her when Yvonne had her first period. It was she who encouraged her when she expressed doubts about her pianistic gifts. She was the one who had performed when Yvonne was had been to play during that fateful concert in Bordeaux on June 6, 1940.

Yvonne continued to remember. Playing four-handed was a pleasure they never deprived themselves of. Whenever they had the chance, in between classes, they would take refuge in the Conservatoire's *Salle Cortot* and enjoyed wholeheartedly time together on the piano. For hours on end, they would play four-handed scores. In fact, that's how they were nicknamed in the corridors of the Conservatoire when you came across them: "Tiens, les quatre mains!" ("Well, here are the four hands!"). But one day, Yvonne saw that Myriam was not the same kind of person she had known before. Her demeanor had become somber. She was not like the shadow of her former self. One by one, she declined Yvonne's invitations, and their four-handed sessions never took place again. Never again did they share this common passion. Their friendship was altered. As the days passed, all "joie de vivre" faded from her once joyful face. A yellow star had been sewn onto her clothes, on her breast ... Later, much later, she learned the rest of what happened to her. A few weeks after the concert, Myriam was among the deportees.

In Yvonne's mind, a "gendarme" was manhandling and violently dragging Myriam back to the group she had run away from. Yvonne gestured to Jean-Pierre, as if hoping he would intervene to help her friend. But, like a furious wave that recedes from the shore and dissolves in the open sea, her remembrance became blurry and vanished ... Meanwhile, Jean-Pierre, who had been watching not knowing what to do make of the strange expressions on Yvonne's face and had sat speechless, spoke up and asked Yvonne,

"Where would you like me to drop you off?"

She responded, saying, "Take me to *Place d'Aligre*."

Staring into space, she spoke up and said:

"I can't help it anyway. It's not my fault. It's their fault ... Their fault!"

Jean-Pierre was intrigued by this final, half-hearted confession, but he didn't let it show. He drove off without a word.

Having reached *Quai de la Rapée*, he drove along *Bassin de l'Arsenal*, and right after entered *Place de la Bastille*, from where he almost immediately exited into *Rue de Charenton* and, three streets further, parked near *Square Trousseau*, next to a police station. Yvonne got out of the cab. After asking him to wait for a moment, she strolled towards *Place d'Aligre*. Jean-Pierre didn't take his eyes off her: this time he told himself that enough was enough, that he had to stop this errand, that he was going to call it a day. Then, one question followed another in his head: *what if she didn't come back, what if she left without paying, what if ... what if ... ?*

Yvonne had walked along the covered market, past the town hall, the *Mairie d'Aligre*—a town hall just for laughs, she told herself—and walked through the square of the same name where the flea market was held every Saturday : a hodgepodge of motley goods on sale for the usual thrifters looking for a good deal; various knick-knacks, postcards from another era, supposedly vintage furniture pieces; all sorts of trinkets that neglect and oblivion had piled up in attics from generation to generation.

At another spot, on an opaque plastic tarpaulin on the ground, a pile of clothes of dubious cleanliness formed an unstable pyramid, around which the thrifters worked and rummaged in the most anarchic fashion. They tossed, turned and even sniffed the clothes, and when they didn't fit—which was almost always the case—they dropped them with an air of disdain. Others, on the other hand, clutched their findings, as if they'd got their hands on a possible "treasure". A few buggers, fairly drunken, were wandering through the market aisles, their eyelids heavy, their complexions gray, dragging their worn-out carcasses. There was not a trace of hope in their eyes.

Yvonne stopped in front of a stall displaying an old typewriter among various antiques. She leaned over, curious about the make—it was a Corona. Her mind flew. She could see the keys of the keyboard pressing in and out on their own, she could hear a jerky metallic clatter, the carriage constantly moving back and forth, as if invisible hands were urgently typing a report that would never end … The second-hand dealer, a giant resembling an authentic Viking, was about to give her the story, but no sooner had he taken a step towards, she at once evaded him with a nervous wave of her hand and turned her head away. She continued on her way.

In front of the convenience store, she stood stunned for a long moment, as when one feels distressed to find oneself in front of a familiar scenery, but which one fails to recognize. As she passed through the entrance, a cold neon light froze her for a few seconds. Her gaze wandered over the surrounding scenery, and her mind was touched by the diffuse memory she had of the place: she was intimately convinced at that point that she was back in the thirties, in a brasserie she remembered vividly.

She could see once again the Art Deco chandeliers hanging from the ceiling and replacing the vulgar neon lights diffusing their bland light. But her imagination didn't stop there, for even as she moved through the aisles of this convenience store, she continued her dreamy way, her memory shaping the scenery as she went. They all had left in a hurry that day... The walls were covered in flaking saltpeter, chairs abandoned on the floor, glasses with dull bowls, a dusty lounge bar, ashtrays overflowing with yellowed cigarette butts, a dirty sink, a pile of dirty plates. She moved slowly, as if sleepwalking, visualizing everything with every step she took. A chair she had just bumped stopped her. *We used to meet here with several friends, after the factory...* she whispered unconsciously. She continued to make her way through the reconstructed setting where she had found herself so many times before. She advanced cautiously, looking lost all around. Suddenly, she froze: a young man, his face emaciated and livid, his lips bloodless, a mute terror in his eyes, was striding slowly towards her. *Isi ... Isi,* she cried, her voice full of emotion. Around her, people were coming and going through the aisles. They were pushing their shopping carts without paying any attention to her or being surprised by her obvious lostness. Yvonne hurried to join him, but found an obstacle in her path that forced her to stop...

4

"Is something wrong, ma'am? Are you feeling unwell?"

A young cashier who had just left her desk to come to her aid now stood beside her and asked, "Would you like me to call a doctor?"

Yvonne, her gaze lost amid the comings and goings of convenience store customers, clearly aching with the high volume of the commercials, winced in pain, squinted in embarrassment and concern at the sight of all the images and noise swirling around her. Worried, she turned to the young woman:

"Who are you? And where are we? This used to be a brasserie, didn't it?"

The young woman didn't know. She was far too young to have any idea. She accompanied her towards the exit, speaking softly to reassure her.

"I'm sure of it," said Yvonne, confused, "there used to be a brasserie here, right here! I've been here many times..."

"Sit down for a moment... Would you like me to get you a glass of water?"

"You're very kind, but—she suddenly remembered it —my taxi is waiting for me. I don't want him to be worried. I must go now."

The young cashier accompanied Yvonne to the exit. She hesitated a moment and then looked gently at the young woman, her eyes full of deep nostalgia.

"I was your age when I used to come here on Saturday nights to dance. But I'm boring you with my stories! We could meet sometime, at my place, and I'll tell you about it if you like..."

She placed a hand gently on the young woman's cheek, gracing her with a tender smile. She added in a low voice:

"You know, I've only loved one man in my life... You're beautiful, I was beautiful too, you know... People used to say that to me..."

Troubled, the young woman gazed at Yvonne's frail silhouette as she was disappearing Place d'Aligre, and overwhelmed by this encounter, she returned to her desk. All the while, Jean-Pierre was doing his best to resist the temptation to drink. His cell phone had rung several times. Eventually, he picked it up and put it on loudspeaker, because of the street noise. It was his ex-wife, Catherine. She'd come to the news:

"Hello? Can you hear me?" His features were frozen. "I know you can hear me! So, I'm warning you, if I haven't received the money by the end of the week, my lawyer will report it to the judge, and then you'll only have your eyes left to cry! They'll seize everything from you, I warn you! They will take everything they can, even your cab. Well, our cab!" she corrected. "Hello, are you listening? Hello? Hello?"

Jean-Pierre didn't think it was worth answering. He hung up. He'd been letting things fall apart over time for a long time now. He immediately took stock of his situation: his money problems, his wife who was threatening him, the rent he hadn't paid yet, his gambling debts, his penchant for alcohol... And that crazy old woman who didn't even know where to go! But his thoughts were interrupted by Yvonne's unexpected return. She was walking up the street towards him, looking totally lost. When she was about twenty meters from the cab, she stopped, questioned a passer-by who replied in the negative, then trotted on.

Jean-Pierre watched her with a mixture of apprehension and amusement. He got out of the cab and waved for her to spot him. She happily did the same. Relieved to have arrived safely, Yvonne settled into the cab, almost perky, as if nothing had happened. Jean-Pierre turned around. This time he wanted to set the record straight.

"Look, all we've been doing since this morning is driving around Paris, here and there, and I still don't know where I'm supposed to take you! I'm beginning to think you don't know yourself..."

He hesitated for a moment. Then, added in a persuasive tone...

"You don't want me to take you home?"

"Take me home? But I don't want to go home! You know, if there's one thing I'm sure of, one thing only, it's that I don't want to go home!"

And, as if this remark almost surprised her, she added, weighing her words:

"Besides, I've never felt at home ... would you mind getting started?" she added impatiently. "I've got the money to pay you, if that's what you're worried about!"

Stunned by this last statement, he hesitated for a second, then made an attempt to calm things down:

"It's not that, Madame. I'm just saying..."

Interrupting him, Yvonne leaned over and spoke into his ear:

"But of course it is... Money is the heart of the matter, isn't it? I know all about that... And here, I'm already going to pay you what I owe you. After that, we'll see."

And before he could reply, she actively rummaged in her bag, pulling out various items, a make-up kit, some old letters stamped with Hitler's effigy, a few photographs and a checkbook; grabbing a pen, she set about writing a check.

"How much do you need?"

Under any other circumstances, Jean-Pierre would have turned her down, but... given his financial situation, he couldn't see himself refusing such an opportunity. To save face, he pretended to hesitate.

"Look, right now, I just need to know where you want to go ... as for the money, we'll see later ..."

"So we're back on the road?" responded Yvonne. "Or have I misunderstood you?

Realizing that he'd just lost the party, Jean-Pierre re-frained from answering and let her detail the program.

She said, "Very well, then. Let's go to *Nation*!"

He sighed and started the car.

5

The cab pulled up alongside Square Trousseau and turned into Rue du Faubourg St-Antoine. On the out-skirts of the Place de la Nation, Jean-Pierre took advan-tage of the stoplight to speak to her again. Almost stammering, he said:

"As for money, I'd rather have cash... You know what I mean?" Yvonne looked at him with a mischievous glance, a slight smile on her lips, but didn't reply.

The traffic light turned green, and the cab resumed its journey.

"There's a post office a little further down the boule-vard, just there, on your left... Drop me off next door, and I'll go and get what I need to pay you."

The cab double-parked on the boulevard. Yvonne got out and jay crossing, she headed directly to the post of-fice. Fearing that she might disappear, Jean-Pierre tried to keep an eye on her, but too late: she was already trot-ting through traffic, and after crossing the street safely, she disappeared from his field of vision. He locked his cab and ran across the street to find her. He entered the post office, surveyed the counters, stared at the customers waiting their turn, and thought aloud:

"This is it! I've just been conned. What an idiot! What an idiot!"

In a daze, he headed back to his cab with the firm intention of driving away, but at that moment he spotted her a few meters away: she was sitting on a public bench, her handbag on her lap, static, absent. He slalomed back across the avenue between the cars to reach her.

Yvonne's face was haggard; lost in her thoughts, she looked like any anonymous, lonely old lady waiting for time to pass. He was surprised to see an immense sadness emanating from her face.

Jean-Pierre approached her, took a seat beside her, and was convinced that something was wrong with her. The shrill sound of the National Emergency Signal siren echoed throughout the street.

"You were right," she said in an atonal tone, "this is Wednesday. You were right..."

"I was convinced you'd left..."

"It was the month of September 1943, I had just turned 21..."

She smiled faintly.

"I arrived in Paris totally destitute. I didn't know a soul. I was lost. I didn't know where to go. I sat there, exactly where we are now, on that bench. I cried for hours, not knowing what to do..."

Her eyelids flooded with tears, she paused for a moment.

"There was still bombing... The siren was wailing, just like now. Everyone was running for the shelters. I didn't have the strength to move, as if subconsciously I wanted everything to stop, for them to take me away, to arrest me... to get it over with..."

Like a hunted animal, with a distraught look in her eyes, she looked around. *Danger could resurface at any moment*, she thought. And through the prism of her memories, the environment changed again: she saw passers-by dressed in the style of the forties; the cars, as well as the buses, were in keeping with that period. Suddenly, she froze : she had just noticed the silhouette of a man in a long leather jacket, identical to that worn by members of the Gestapo, coming towards them. She intuitively took refuge, as a frightened child would, and huddled against Jean-Pierre's shoulder. But the man passed her by; in fact, he was dressed quite normally and in a contemporary style.

Yvonne watched the man walk away without understanding, and continued her story, occasionally turning briefly to Jean-Pierre, looking lost: "I was cold. I was thinking: *My God, why have you abandoned me!* Then a gentleman elegantly dressed came forward. He asked me why I was crying. I told him my fear: the fear of never being able to sit and the piano again. He spoke softly to reassure me and offered to buy me a hot chocolate as to warm me up until the end of the alert; it was right there in that café..."

She nodded and Jean-Pierre followed her gesture and indeed noticed a café on the corner of the avenue.

She continued:

"He wrote down a friend's address on a piece of paper, and said she'd help me find a place to stay. Then he handed me his business card, a hundred-franc bill so I could take a cab to his friend's house, and left, smiling at me one last time. I never saw that man again... I did as he said: I got in touch with his friend; she took me in, and then found me a job. Exactly where we were this morning, at the Panhard factory..."

Suddenly she changed her tone and demeanor:

"But everything's fine now! I've been waiting for you too! By the way—she spoke while she was happily patting her handbag—I haven't forgotten you!"

She took out an envelope made of craft paper and opened it. Jean-Pierre glimpsed at the stack of bills and immediately put his hand down to interrupt her gesture.

"Not now!" he said, casting a worried glance around him.

"Why not now? Are you afraid people will think you're a gigolo? She laughed at her own audacity. Let's go, I can't wait to get on the road ; when you're rolling, you forget everything! Don't you forget everything, Jean-Pierre?"

It was the first and only time she called him by his first name. And he, without understanding why, felt flattered. Yvonne stared at him, waiting for him to answer, but he remained stoic. He was reflecting on what he had just heard: *When you're on the road, you forget everything...* Wasn't that his fundamental problem?

Elegantly, he offered her his arm to help her stand up. It amused him to play the servant knight. They crossed the avenue, while she said, "We're going to have a wonderful trip... We're going to have a lovely trip, aren't we?"

At the word "trip", Jean-Pierre started to be concerned: *What more surprises does she have in store for me? Now, it's all about traveling!*

After crossing the avenue, they got into the cab. Yvonne insisted he take the envelope. Jean-Pierre discovered that it contained a very large sum of money, much more than he had imagined.

"Why are you giving me so much? I don't need all this! Just give me what you owe me for now and keep the rest!"

"Taratata," she replied, pushing his hand away, "I can assure you that you'll need it. I know what I'm talking about..."

He put the envelope back in the glove compartment, turned on the ignition, hesitated for a moment, then turned off the engine. Something was bothering him...

"What you mean by having a nice trip, I don't quite understand."

"But I've already told you. I don't know myself... Get going! We'll see about that later..."

And when he didn't react, she felt obligated to add:

"Since you want to know everything, I need to see places I've loved. Quite simply... places I'll probably never see again, friends I've lost sight of and would like to see again. Some of them are already hoping to see

35

me! At my age, you'll have to admit that I don't have much time left... Of course, as I've promised you, I'll pay you whatever it takes—that goes without saying! This trip is just a matter of a few days..."

Jean-Pierre gasped: "A few days!"

With an enigmatic smile, Yvonne nodded. He adjusted his rearview mirror:

"Let's say I accept your proposal... You promise there won't be any problems?"

Jean-Pierre's naive attempt amused her: she understood that he was about to give in. To convince him completely, she nodded and gave him a smile.

Jean-Pierre pondered aloud:

"I need to think... I've got to get organized..."

He added, doubtful:

"Did you say a few days? Can't you be more precise?"

"Well, I don't know. How long does it take to get to Biarritz?"

"Biarritz!"

"Yes, Biarritz. What's wrong with that? Don't you like Biarritz?"

Jean-Pierre couldn't suppress a smile: she'd just spoke with such assurance! And candor!

"But why didn't you tell me this morning? It's going to cost a fortune!"

"Fortune favors the bold!" she replied.

Then she added:

"If I had told you earlier, I'm not sure you would have accepted. Would you have accepted?"

Without waiting for an answer, she exclaimed,

"So, how much is it going to cost?"

"I don't know... I'd say... one thousand five hundred... two thousand euros or so; plus travel expenses, of course. I can offer you a package deal..."

"That's very kind of you. I'd be delighted. In any case, money is not an issue for me."

"For a long-distance trip," responded Jean-Pierre, "I'll have to make my own arrangements. I've got to make a phone call to get organized. I'll just be a minute..."

He stopped the taxi meter, and once out on the street, he isolated himself to take stock. He had to face the facts: this errand was a godsend and just in time. Why turn it down? This unexpected windfall of cash could help him avoid the worst in the immediate future and allow him to get back on his feet. After speaking on the phone, he resumed his place at the wheel and started the engine.

"It's all arranged. I'm going home to pick up a few things. I won't be long..."

"I've got plenty of time..." she said, pleased to have won the game.

6

Suburbs of *Clichy-la-Garenne*. Jean-Pierre parked near a small, dilapidated building adjoining a vacant lot. He walked towards the building, hesitated for a moment, retraced his steps, and advised Yvonne to wait for him in the car. She nodded in agreement, and watched Jean-Pierre enter the building.

In a studio apartment on the first floor, his silhouette reappeared as a shadowy figure behind a window, obscured by a veil. The remnants of an old shop, the studio was spartanly furnished: a checkout counter served as a desk, a slate holding a reminder list, a mattress laid out on pallets. Jean-Pierre took a few items of clothing from a shelf, quickly stuffed them into a bag, added a few useful accessories (a cell phone charger, a thermos flask, a road map, a toiletry kit), then glanced outside. He parted a curtain, worried about what Yvonne might be doing in his absence. He saw her putting on her make-up: she was applying lipstick, pinching her upper lip and smoothing it over her lower lip. Reassured, he finished filling his bag, exited the building and froze:

the car door was open, and Yvonne had vanished! Jean-Pierre set off in search of her, and found her a few yards further away, at the edge of a building site fence. She was picking wild flowers, humming a sort of nursery rhyme from another time.

"What in the world are you doing?"

"What kind of question is that? A flower bouquet, of course! Isn't it obvious? And what were you doing? What took you so long? I was bored, so I took the opportunity to relax …"

She smilingly handed the bouquet to Jean-Pierre, who had no choice but to take it. Looking annoyed, he headed for his cab. She followed close behind, still humming the same tune. He opened the back door, inviting her to sit, and deposited her bag and bouquet in the trunk. As he programmed his GPS, Yvonne tapped his shoulder insistently. Annoyed, he turned around.

"Don't you like flowers?"

"What?"

"Don't you like flowers? If you did, you'd never have put them in the trunk!"

Jean-Pierre realized he had no choice: he went to get the bouquet from the trunk, upset but controlling himself. Yvonne was jubilant: she'd just had the last word. Suddenly, however, she was startled: Jean-Pierre had just slammed the trunk shut. He returned and carelessly placed the bouquet on the front seat. Yvonne withdrew in herself, brooding. He really didn't like flowers! At his wit's end, Jean-Pierre turned and glared at her:

"Next time you leave without warning, I'll take you home!"

Then he added:

"Do you have a preference for the route?"

"I'm not sure … What I do know is that I hate the freeway! I'd rather we took the small country roads. Aren't small roads charming?"

Jean-Pierre simply rolled his eyes and started off.

7

Reluctantly, Jean-Pierre followed Yvonne's recommendation to the letter. For some sixty kilometers, he took the back roads. But when he reached *Rambouillet* and noticed that she had dozed off, he didn't hesitate for a second and got on the freeway as soon as possible. After an hour, the constant speed and monotonous landscape produced a weariness in him that he could no longer fight. From time to time, to keep himself awake, he glanced at his rearview mirror to see if Yvonne was still asleep. Her head was resting against the window, and her face seemed soothed. Yet, in her sleep, she was stammering confused words, difficult to hear. After trying to decipher these babblings, Jean-Pierre let out a deep yawn and had to concentrate to avoid sinking further into a drowsiness he knew he couldn't control for much longer. He saw a sign indicating a rest area and decided to stop. He turned into the right-hand lane, drove past the gas pumps, and parked in the parking lot next to the store. Before getting out, he made sure Yvonne was still asleep, stepped outside and gently closed the car door to avoid waking her. After stretching to relax, he took in the sights and whistled his way to the store. It had been a long time since he'd been in such a carefree mood. He felt … yes, light, free of all the worries that had long been his daily lot. With a final, liberating yawn, he slipped some change into the hot-beverage dispenser and pressed the extended-coffee button. As his cup filled up, he glanced outside to make sure Yvonne was still in the car. He headed for the exit to be sure, but distracted by the beep that warned him his order was ready, he stepped back. He picked up his cup, stepped outside, stirring his coffee, and then stopped dead in his tracks: the back door of the cab was open. Yvonne had disappeared! The heat of the cup burned his hand and he dropped it. He tried to catch it, but it slipped out of his hand and fell on the floor. He swore, wiped his face and set off to find Yvonne at the rest area. He came up empty. Back in the store, he inspected the ladies' toilets, and came face to face with a lady giving herself a makeover. She glared at him:

"The men's room … It's next door!" she said gruffly.

He returned to the parking lot. Yvonne was just a few yards away: she was sitting at a concrete picnic table under a tree, in the company of an old man of about seventy, laughing and talking volubly. She seemed oblivious to Jean-Pierre's presence. But after a while, she beckoned him over:

"It's incredible! Come over here! Let me introduce you to someone …"

Jean-Pierre took a few steps and remained at a distance to show his annoyance.

"Roger, this is Jean-Pierre, my chauffeur ..."

The man held out a filthy hand and said, "My dear sir, how delighted I am to meet you ..." An old-fashioned way to speak and show politeness, to say the least, thought Jean-Pierre. This greeting failed to strike a chord with Jean-Pierre. He remained unmoved. Annoyed at having been called a chauffeur, furious that Yvonne had become infatuated with the first man to come along in his absence, he fulminated in the presence of this ... He couldn't think of a nickname to match the phenomenon and, after observing him from head to toe, decided to call him a vagabond. Yes, vagabond suited him very well: stocky, short, the man wore worn-out slippers, a filthy jogging suit, topped by an old, oversized sweater, also of very relative cleanliness ... His hands, which were particularly large, had long fingers with blistered nails, and seemed to indicate that the man was suffering from some pathology. On his slumped face, small eyes sunken in disproportionate sockets constantly darted from left to right, giving him a particularly worrying look.

"Jean-Pierre, we've got to help this gentleman," said Yvonne, as he stared at the man. "For God's sake, come closer! You're making me dizzy just standing there!"

Yvonne waited for Jean-Pierre to come closer and added:

"Two days ago, Roger was traveling with his son-in-law and daughter-in-law. He went away for a few minutes to satisfy some … natural needs, and when he came back to the car, they'd gone. Who knows, maybe they forgot him on purpose … Do you know what they call him around here?

Jean-Pierre nodded to say no—They call him *Slippers*! People are so mean … Since then, poor Roger has been wandering around like a lost soul with no one to help him. We're not going to leave him there, are we!"

During Yvonne's outcry, Roger had taken on a victim's posture, showing the facial expression of a spaniel about to be abandoned. As for Jean-Pierre, he remained stoic: he didn't trust this fellow ….

"And … what does this have to do with me !"

"Please don't say that! We can't leave him to his fate! We've got to help him get back home! Jean-Pierre, I beg you!"

Jean-Pierre weighed up the pros and cons, and sighing eloquently, said:

"Well, I suggest we drop this gentleman off at a train station. But that's it! That's the end of it!"

Having said that, he headed for his cab, closely followed by Yvonne and her new protégé. Too happy to have received some pity, the man was chatting with Yvonne as if nothing had happened, holding her familiarly by the shoulder, whispering sweet nothings in her ear.

8

Annoyed by the intruder's presence, Jean-Pierre scowled. He regretted having had the weakness to give in, and promised himself that, in the future, he would never again accept his customer's whims, no matter what. As he ruminated, he wasn't immediately aware of what was happening in the back seat ....

Slippers had made himself at home: he kept whispering things in Yvonne's ear that seemed to be making her more and more uncomfortable. Jean-Pierre glanced in the rearview mirror to check that all was well, just as the man was wrapping his large palms around Yvonne's head to force her to kiss him. Jean-Pierre immediately performed a perilous maneuver: he slammed his car into the emergency lane. Once out, he had to brace himself against the door to avoid being snatched up by a truck swiftly passing by. With the danger averted, he sped around his cab, opened the rear door and vigorously ejected the old man, who left running and shouting sexist insults at Yvonne. Jean-Pierre moved a few steps in his direction, but quickly gave up pursuing him. He climbed back into his cab and set off again.

In the back seat, Yvonne was having a hard time: she was looking through the rear window at Roger's silhouette, which was getting smaller by the minute, thinking: *I couldn't have known. I thought I was doing the right thing ....*

Furious, with a defeated look on his face, Jean-Pierre scolded her:

"Madame, I'm a cab driver. I'm not a social worker!"

Yvonne didn't reply. She just seemed to be taking it all in as she nodded her head mechanically.

"See if he's stolen anything," said Jean-Pierre. Yvonne was looking around to check.

"My bag! He's taken my bag!" she suddenly exclaimed ....

Jean-Pierre scrambled to pull over. He ran to catch up with the man, but by the time he reached the spot where they had parked a short while ago, the cars were moving so fast that he gave up, fearing that *Slippers* would decide to cross on the other side of the road. Aware that the man's chances of survival would be virtually nil, Jean-Pierre didn't want to push him into a corner. Two hundred meters away, Roger stood hesitating and waiting for the traffic to ease before crossing. For a few seconds, his gaze shifted from the road in front of him to his pursuer to assess his chances. Suddenly, he took advantage of a relative lull in traffic and embarked on a perilous crossing. Motorists, seeing this figure appear from nowhere, started braking and changing lanes to avoid mowing him down. Against all odds, *Slippers* managed to cross safely to the other side. Jean-Pierre, reassured to see him straddle the guardrails, watched him disappear into a forest of cornfield stalks.

On the way back, he found Yvonne's bag, which the man had abandoned during his run, and further on, a few photos, several envelopes, various knick-knacks which he didn't have time to sort through, and finally a letter from Biarritz Town Hall which he hastened to look at and containing information about a procedure concerning a house belonging to Yvonne.

Dear Madam,

You own a house, 6 bis rue Ambroise Paré, in Biarritz. We would like to inform you that this house presents the following problems:

1/Risk of a falling wall.
2/Risk of falling tiles
3/Risk of roof collapse.

This situation is likely to result in the opening of a peril decree procedure, in accordance with articles L011-1 and L511-2 of the French Building Code. In accordance with these provisions, I would ask you to inform me within two months of the measures you intend to take to prevent the above-mentioned dangers.

*If you fail to do so, I shall be obliged to issue
a "arrêté de péril" (Danger order). This will
contain an injunction to carry out the work
necessary to put an end to the dangers
caused by the condition of your house ....
Please, etc.*

Yvonne was watching Jean-Pierre through the rear window.

She saw him put back surreptitiously what he had collected in the handbag. Aware that he was being watched, Jean-Pierre held the bag out to give the impression that he was not doing something wrong, but Yvonne was not fooled: she knew that he had accessed the contents of her bag. Jean-Pierre thought he had learned more about her, and Yvonne imagined what he might have discovered. She knew she'd have to tell him the truth at some point. She couldn't escape it. She just had to have the courage ....

When Jean-Pierre got into the car, she acted as if nothing had happened. He handed her back her bag.

"Make sure nothing's missing," he said glumly.

She inspected the contents:

"No ... I don't see ... Oh yes, he stole my make-up bag! I've got to buy a new one! Get off the freeway as soon as possible!"

Jean-Pierre raised his eyebrows in astonishment.

"With you, there's never a dull moment! Are you sure nothing else is missing? I mean, nothing important?"

"No … well, it's hard to tell …"

"Are you sure?"

"Yes, the rest is there."

Jean-Pierre was thinking and hesitating to ask her to explain what he thought he'd discovered. He took the fast lane and headed for the freeway.

Daylight was slowly fading. The sky had that soft, orange color of autumn before the sun sets. The cab turned off at the exit in the direction of Châtellerault[3]

---

[3]*Châtellerault. Town in the Vienne département, Nouvelle Aquitaine région, West-central France. It lies north-northeast of Poitiers on the main road from Paris to Bordeaux.*

9

On a street with no cars and reserved for pedestrians, Jean-Pierre waits outside a perfume shop. Through the shop window, he sees Yvonne buying her make-up kit, while chatting happily with the sales assistant. As this drags on, Jean-Pierre is becoming impatient. He looks around. On the opposite sidewalk, the sign of a PMU (a betting and gambling shop that also sells cigarettes) catches his eye. He quickly turns his head away from the sign.

Voluble, Yvonne is always talking ….

He's lost so much in gambling, lost so much!

Yvonne holds a hairbrush in one hand, feels it with the other, hesitates ….

Jean-Pierre knows only too well that gambling and drinking are his demons ….

For Yvonne, cost was not an issue: she wants the best quality ….

Jean-Pierre peers through the window. The atmosphere is friendly, with everyone's eyes fixed on the plasma screen; he can't stop thinking that, having lost so often, his chances of winning can only increase. It's mathematical! He turns to see if Yvonne is finished: but no, still not! She's still roaming the aisles of the perfume shop, the saleswoman in her wake ....

He feels the weight of the envelope Yvonne has given him in his pocket; he hasn't counted, but from the looks of it, there's enough, and without compromising the future, he thinks ....

He enters the bar and joins a group of overexcited turf players, their eyes fixed on the screen. Confident, he deposits a hundred-euro bill in front of the cashier; it's a big bet, the horse is an old acquaintance and the distance suits him particularly well. But on reflection, he hesitates, changes his mind. The horses are in the starting stalls. The sudden silence freezes the atmosphere. Suddenly in doubt, he rushes back to the ticket office and places half the contents of the envelope on the race. His intuition tells him that this time it's the right one. He feels it intensely. One can't explain it. It has to be part of a lived experience ....

Yvonne stands at the cash register. She pays for her purchases, looking delighted. She exits and joins Jean Pierre. He looks like a child, a "petite mine", as they say. Yvonne blames herself for having spent almost an hour on purchases that suddenly seem trivial.

Jean-Pierre holds the steering wheel with a stiffened hand, his attitude as if crushed; he is still replaying the gloomy assessment of his day and the film of his failure: his favorite, about to win, swerved, and the jockey fell two meters from the finish line. Two meters! Of course, he had wanted to make up for it in the next race. And he had indeed been redone. At the point he'd reached, this remark carved a sardonic smile on the bottom of his face. The content of the envelope was gone. The whole envelope! He'd been born cursed, that's for sure, nothing would ever work out for him, nothing, nothing, nothing!

Upon Yvonne's advice, he set off for *Genillé*, an ancient village. In the back seat, Yvonne gazes out the window at the landscape. With the speed, the trees lining the road produce a stroboscopic effect. Dizzy with the movement, she closes her eyes. But lest her mind wander back to the past, she immediately opens them again and rolls down her window. Fresh air rushes into the cabin and whips across her face. The kinetic illusion finally fades.

"Jean-Pierre. I hope you don't mind about what happened earlier?"

Jean-Pierre glanced at the rearview mirror.

"What are you talking about?"

"About making you wait outside the perfume shop …"

By way of reply, Jean-Pierre raised his eyebrows in astonishment. Yvonne interpreted this gesture as a sign of forgiveness.

Reassured, she took out her brand-new make-up kit and put on her perfume. She began to apply her carmine lipstick. After spreading, it roughly over her lips, she curled her upper lip over her lower lip and executed a burlesque grimace to distribute the excess lipstick harmoniously. But it overflowed so grossly around the corners that her face now resembled that of a sad clown. She continued the operation, powdering her cheeks generously, producing a cloud of powder that spread throughout the cab's cabin. Brought back to reality by this rather ridiculous scene, Jean-Pierre had to dust his face with his hand to dissipate the untimely cloud. He bit his lower lip to keep from laughing.

Yvone thought, *What's so funny about that? You can be a certain age and still be "coquette"!*

After a few more kilometers, she pointed out the hamlet she wanted to go to:

"You'll see when you come out of the next village, you'll turn right. I'll tell you when …"

Then she added:

"We'll go through a short detour. Then I'll take you to a little inn I know."

"Very well, Madame," said Jean-Pierre, playing the role of a chauffeur.

Yvonne reacted, saying, "Stop making fun of me! And stop calling me Madame! I'd prefer you to call me Yvonne … or Mademoiselle if you prefer. That said, I don't mind music …"

"Well, Mademoiselle …" he said, a touch of irony in his voice.

Jean-Pierre flipped through several stations, settling on one that played jazz standards. Then, in a tone meant to be appropriate, he added:

"Is that all right with you?"

"By the way, is your name Jean-Pierre? Isn't it?" Asked Yvonne.

"Yes, it hasn't changed since this morning …"

"You don't have to act like my chauffeur!" replied Yvonne.

"Isn't that what I am?"

"I prefer to think of you as my companion. And for that, I thank you sincerely."

Jean-Pierre appreciated the remark and gave a friendly smile in the rearview mirror.

"Am I accompanying you or keeping you company?" asked Jean-Pierre.

Yvonne was deep in her thoughts. She didn't answer. She took refuge in contemplation of the scenery. Jean-Pierre, satisfied that he'd had the last word, was beginning to feel that the trip was taking a more pleasant turn. Or so he thought ….

"Jean-Pierre?"

"Yes …"

"Why did you agree to drive me to Biarritz?"

"I'm doing my job …"

"Well, yes, but … was nothing keeping you in Paris? Well, I don't know … Don't you have …"

"A wife, children, a dog? No, I don't have anyone. Well, not anymore … If you don't mind, I'd rather talk about something else …"

"You do have one friend, don't you?"

"Yes. Her name is Mademoiselle Yvonne!"

"You're silly!"

"Shall we go for a little speed?"

"If you like."

With his foot to the floor, Jean-Pierre kept his word: the acceleration was powerful. Yvonne found herself glued to the back of her seat. Intoxicated by the speed, she closed her eyes to savor the moment. In the distance, one could make out a hamlet. As it approached, the cab resumed its cruising speed. The sky was beginning to be filled with clouds. Like under the effect of a solar eclipse, the surrounding countryside was plunged into sudden darkness.

"Would you turn the lights on?" said Yvonne in a small voice.

Her face now looked crumpled. Jean-Pierre turned on the ceiling light. Dazzled, Yvonne blinked for a few moments, until she became accustomed to the light.

"What was your happiest day?" she asked softly.

"My happiest day … I think it was when I was a child. I was uncertain about everything. The origin of life, the immensity of the universe, and so much more. In short, all the questions a child might have about the world he discovers. But I sensed that something was different … something I still can't explain to myself today … a sort of mixed feeling of disquiet and wonder … like the miraculous sensation of being alive. You know what I mean? The truth is, I don't know how to explain it …"

He noticed Yvonne's attentive expression in the rearview mirror and responded, "You describe it very well … You felt you existed. A feeling of being alive. Simply alive, isn't that right?"

"Yes, perhaps. I don't know, maybe … That must be it."

There was a silence, each one being immersed in memories of their youth. Jean-Pierre resumed softly:

"I think I felt a kind of fear … a fear mixed with wonder. Yes, in the end you're right: I felt alive! Today, it's different … It's all gone, and now it's just a pain in the ass, if you'll pardon the expression! What was your happiest day?"

He looked up at the rearview mirror. Mademoiselle's face was beginning to take on a slightly nostalgic cast.

"My happiest day …" she said dreamily, without elaborating.

Jean-Pierre turned off the ceiling light. In the shadows, Yvonne remembered an evening in the spring of 1940 ….

She'd been to the Royal cinema in Biarritz with Isi. They watched "Battement de cœur", a film by Henri Decoin. She loved the story of the young orphan, Arlette, who escapes from a boarding school and finds herself alone, penniless, in a hostile Paris. The young woman meets Monsieur Aristide who runs a special kind of school, the art of becoming a pickpocket … Yvonne had promised herself that evening that she too would run away one day ….

Throughout the movie, Yvonne had left her hand on the armrest, palm open, offered, in the hope that Isi would take it. But he hadn't dared.

As they left the cinema, his eyes downcast, Isi had offered to accompany her home. They climbed up to the top of the *Plage des Basques*. On the way back, Yvonne grabbed his hand and squeezed it tight. She didn't let go until they reached the stairs leading down to the beach. They kissed for the first time. Their eyes were closed, their lips half-open, shy and inexperienced. Both shivered with emotion, lulled by the crash of the waves on the rocks below. Their lips remained joined for a long moment.

That night, Yvonne couldn't sleep. She replayed over and over the magical moment she had just experienced for the first time.

Jean-Pierre turned on the headlights. The cab sped along the winding road as they approached the hamlet.

10

The cab pulled into what appeared to be the main square, and parked close to a ruined, burnt-out house. Yvonne, holding a faded bouquet of flowers—the one she'd composed that morning in Clichy—stepped out of the cab and followed the headlights towards the ruin. With difficulty, she pushed open the wrought-iron gate. Her shadow, cast on the front of the house, showed her hesitating. Then her silhouette disappeared completely, escaping Jean-Pierre's gaze for a few moments. She climbed a few steps and found herself at the edge of a garden invaded by wild, luxuriant vegetation. Fascinated by the place, she observed the remains of the building. She was gradually overwhelmed by fleeting, violent images: hurried footsteps, the sound of car doors, orders uttered in German … She bent down, ceremoniously placed the bouquet of flowers on the top of the steps, then turned back. As she turned back, Yvonne stumbled and staggered. Jean-Pierre rushed over and helped her to her feet. When she was settled in the cab, he started driving. Looking through the window, she seemed to be searching the deep darkness with her eyes, mumbling Isi's name without realizing it. They drove through the deserted hamlet. The headlights intermittently scanned the signs of shops with their shutters permanently closed. As they left the hamlet, the cab turned right onto a main road surrounded by freshly plowed fields. Faint traces of mist floated above the still damp earth.

"What happened in that house? Earlier, I heard you calling … Isi … Was Isi your friend?" asked Jean-Pierre.

Yvonne remained silent. *No, I won't tell him what happened here … He'd think I was crazy!*

And with a trembling voice, she whispered, "Would you turn on the heating, please? I'm freezing to death!"

Jean-Pierre was waiting for an answer, but Yvonne remained silent. He complied, making a last attempt:

"You know, when you don't answer my questions, it makes me uncomfortable …"

They came to an intersection that served two roads. Jean-Pierre hesitated and pulled over. He switched on the ceiling light and turned back to Yvonne. Dazzled, she looked at him and blinked.

He asked, "Which road do I take now? The one on the right or the one on the left?"

There was a long silence where only Yvonne's breathing seemed to be present. In a soft voice, she replied:

"Take the road on your right. That's where we're going."

Jean-Pierre sighed wearily. He turned off the over-head light and set off on the narrow, winding road that climbed up to the heights. It seemed to lead nowhere. A light fog had rolled in, forcing him to drive slowly. After a few kilometers, through the fog, the inn finally appeared, as if floating in midair.

"Was it in the village where we were staying that you met your friend?"

"No, the first time I met him was at the conservatory in Bayonne. I think I remember it was in 1939 … He was studying violin. I knew that because I'd often come across him in the corridors of the conservatory with his case, which he held tightly. He was always alone. He never spoke to anyone. But I didn't know him then. Later, we met at a competition in the chamber music class.

We had to prepare a work by *Sarasate* [4] for violin and piano: *Das Zigeunerweisen.* Do you know it?"

Jean-Pierre, who was listening attentively, met her eyes and nodded no. Yvonne softly hummed some parts of the work.

"This music is wonderful …" she said with emotion. "I remember our first rehearsal. Isi didn't dare speak to me … Whenever I looked at him, he looked away. He was terribly shy. I had the impression that he had a panic fear of the world around him … He was clumsy too!

---

[4]*Pablo de Sarasate* was a Spanish violinist and composer, born in Pamplona on March 10, 1844, and died in Biarritz on September 20, 1908. He was one of the most virtuosic violinists of his time.

One day when we were playing, his foot caught on a strip of the wooden floor, and he went sprawling all over the place, flat on his back … As he fell, he instinctively held out his arm to protect his violin. He remained motionless, as if frozen … Alerted by the noise, a teacher entered the room and caught him in this posture. I laughed to see the teacher's bewildered face, who scolded us and left. Isi stood up. He looked at me as if guilty, and we resumed our rehearsal. He played with such ardor, passion and incredible freedom, without restraint. I felt as if his violin was proclaiming everything he couldn't communicate. Rarely have I seen a performer being metamorphosed to such an extent …"

Yvonne paused for a moment. She was smiling wistfully. A smile lost in the limbo of the past which, for once, brought her an ounce of sweetness. Jean-Pierre, touched to see her open up so freely, couldn't believe his eyes.

"Sometimes, after rehearsing," she continued, "we'd take refuge behind the conservatory, out of sight. We'd embrace for long moments. We didn't speak. Nothing existed but the two of us. I could feel his warm, wet breath on my neck. I tried to match my breathing to his … At first, it was like a game. Then, day by day, these moments became mysterious, troubling … We made a promise to each other: we'd stay together for the rest of our lives, no matter what. It was no joke! We were young, but we were serious! Very soon, we had to see each other in secret because my father forbade me to see him outside the conservatory because Isi was Jewish! So, whenever we could, we'd meet up on the main beach, or on the beach at Port-Vieux. But then … And then it became too risky for his family to stay in Biarritz. The Germans were everywhere by then. His family moved to this village where we were just now, and we lost touch with each other. Later, I learned that they had all been deported and that their house had been burnt down … I suspected my father of having betrayed them to the Germans. I could never prove it … But I had a front-row seat: I knew my father's ideas and his connections …"

"Since we left Paris," interjected Jean-Pierre "This is the first time you've confided in me like this. And your friend, Isi … You've never seen him again?"

"No, I haven't. He must be decrepit today! Don't you think?"

Jean-Pierre briefly turned his head sideways to look at Yvonne with a shocked expression. Her sudden lightness surprised him, but also amused him.

"Do you think he's still with us?" added Jean-Pierre, looking up at the rearview mirror.

"Maybe he is … Who knows …" she said mysteriously.

But Isi was alive and well, and Yvonne knew it. Admittedly, she hadn't known it for a long time, but now she knew. Only a few weeks ago, she'd received a letter from him in which he confided that he'd been looking for her all those years the war had kept them apart. In the twilight of his life, he wanted to reconnect with her. Reconnect! She found the formula so appallingly banal that she had hesitated whether to destroy the letter. However, something mysterious had prevented her from doing so: a kind of inner voice urged her to reply and not to ignore him ... and so she continued reading. Isi confided in her that he had returned to Biarritz. He ended his letter by telling her that he wanted to spend the rest of his life with her. But Yvonne still hesitated. Finally, she replied with a note promising to come and visit him if the opportunity arose. Such an unkind message, in view of the mutual passion they had felt in their youth, was closely linked to the prospect of this possible reunion. For several weeks, torn by the idea of whether or not to reunite with this love from the past, Yvonne had tried to forget him. Then one day, she finally made up her mind: she would join him and spend the rest of her life with him in Biarritz ....

Yvonne leaned forward on the driver's seat:

"We make a great team, don't we?" she said cheerfully. "At my age, it's not for everyone to walk around with a handsome man!"

Jean-Pierre, flattered by the remark, laughed and smiled heartily.

1940. Yvonne is playing *Schubert's Sonata 20 in A major*. It's part of the program she's soon to play in Bordeaux, at the conservatory's end-of-year concert. She hears strange noises coming from the cellar. She tries to ignore them but can't concentrate. She wants to know. She opens the door beneath the staircase and descends. At the bottom of the stairs, there's a corridor. In the middle, a lamp dangles. Cobwebs everywhere. A pervasive smell of earth and mold.

She makes her way along, following the noise coming from the back. She finds her father tinkering: he's sealing bars to the window overlooking the garden. On a table, there are lots of strange objects: pliers connected to electric wires which are in turn connected to a sort of battery ....

"What's all this, Dad? What's it for? Why are you putting up bars?"

Her father turns around:

"What are you doing here! Go back and work on your piano!"

Yvonne insists, intrigued.

"It's for my wine. I don't want it stolen, so I'm protecting it ... Go back upstairs, I tell you!"

Yvonne won't learn more. In the living room, she gets back to work. But the piano doesn't sound right. She lost her concentration and plays without conviction, mechanically.

11

They arrived at the inn in the dark of night. After settling into their respective rooms, they met for dinner. In the dining room, the presence of a few couples not speaking to each other set the tone for a hushed, provincial atmosphere. A young waitress—strangely wearing stiletto heels—went from table to table, satisfying the small crowd with her somewhat bouncy, sonorous footsteps.

During the meal, Jean-Pierre didn't touch his plate, but looked straight at Yvonne. Troubled by his silence, Yvonne avoided meeting his gaze; she chewed each mouthful long and mechanically, as if harking back to a grudge. Tired of this sullen mood, she beckoned to the waitress, who stepped forward with that peculiar awkwardness so typical of novices in this profession. Yvonne ordered half a bottle of wine. Upon her return, the waitress began to uncork the bottle, slowly and with difficulty. When it came time for Jean-Pierre to taste the wine, he refused. He covered his glass with the palm of his hand and spoke of going to bed.

"Please stay a little longer …" said Yvonne as if apologizing.

For some time, Jean-Pierre's gaze had been drawn to a tattoo on Yvonne's left forearm, forming a series of numbers. It looked like a deportee's identifying number; unlike those used to identify deportees as soon as they arrived in the camps, this one didn't droop at all: the number had regular contours, as if it had been made only a short time ago, a world away from the barbaric technique used in those days.

Jean-Pierre reached for his phone, ready to take a picture. Yvonne immediately moved her sleeve as to hide the phone, and angrily shouted:

"I forbid you to do that!"

"Why not?"

"I have my reasons. Don't take any photos!" she ordered.

Jean-Pierre put his phone back on the table. He raised his hands in a gesture of appeasement.

"Forgive me if I've upset you …"

Yvonne regained her composure. She tried to lighten the mood:

"Don't you think I've upset *you* enough?" she said mischievously.

As he remained silent, she continued:

"Tell me more about yourself, instead of playing the reporter."

Jean-Pierre didn't want to talk about himself. He would have liked to know the origin of the tattoo. Why had she reacted so violently to it?

"I have this tattoo, so I don't forget … you understand? I have it, so I don't forget what I've seen, what I've lived through, what I was too, in spite of myself. During the war, my father chose his side. I was young, and I didn't want to see what was happening around me. All my life, I've never forgiven myself for what I became by his side … I could probably have saved a few Jews, if I hadn't been so weak. But I did nothing. I did nothing. I was afraid. I was terrified. I had a front-row seat, and I couldn't save a single Jew. Their faces haunt me today. Their eyes look at me and will look at me until I die. This tattoo is there so I'll never forget."

Jean-Pierre was pale. He was starting to feel nauseous … He tried to stand up but fell back in his chair. Yvonne poured him a glass of water, which he drank slowly. After thanking her, his gaze turned back to the counter and the waitress. She met his gaze and looked away. She was pretending to be busy.

"I think the waitress is listening …"

"You're the first person I've dared to confide in … Towards the end of the war, I …"

Jean-Pierre looked with intrigue at Yvonne's lips, but he could no longer hear a single sound. Was she still evoking that sad period of her life? His ears were still ringing with what he had just learned about Yvonne. For her part, Yvonne realized he was no longer listening to her and raised her voice.

"Do you know what saved me, Jean-Pierre?"

He was startled and nodded.

"It … is the kindness of people."

Why did she feel obligated to tell him all this? Overwhelmed by all these questions, Jean-Pierre no longer felt strong enough to stay. He wanted to leave, to flee, to take refuge in his room; he didn't want to hear any more of these confessions that had troubled him. He thought about driving away without stopping. He wanted to run away from this woman; escape her guilt. Escape her regrets.

"Yvonne," said Jean-Pierre uneasily. "Forgive me, but I'm in no condition to listen to you anymore. I'm really not …" he mumbled in a tired voice. Then he stood up.

"Wait a minute! Wait a minute! Do you want to know why I'm making this trip?"

Jean-Pierre fell back in his chair. A sigh from him, the outline of a gesture, would have invited Yvonne to confide in him, but nothing in his behavior encouraged her to do so. Jean-Pierre leaned towards Yvonne. He mumbled:

"I think you look sad when you eat. You really do look sad … Everything you tell me is sad too, and I'm tired …"

"Old people look sad when they eat …" said Yvonne, leaning. "If you must know, I'm having trouble chewing. I have to concentrate, that's all."

Jean-Pierre held back a skeptical grin. She sensed that he wasn't fooled and wanted to confide in him further:

"You know, since we left Paris, I've thought about a lot of things … faces, people I've loved, places with people I thought I'd never see again … and it's all thanks to you … without you, I'd …".

She paused: Jean-Pierre's forbidding gaze was discouraging her from continuing.

He was thinking back to what she had said earlier. He was surprised to see that her tone was almost light, relaxed, as if she'd forgotten everything about the past she had remembered.

In a calm voice, Yvonne spoke again:

"Every day I wonder why I'm still here … It's silly, these unanswered questions … Don't you think?"

"What's silly is stirring it all up … It leads nowhere …" muttered Jean-Pierre.

Yvonne looked puzzled, as if she didn't understand. Hesitating between guilt and concern, the expression on her face was that of someone about to confess something unmentionable. So, she took refuge in her thoughts and nibbled sadly at a piece of cheese still lying on her plate. Jean-Pierre, for his part, had given up questioning her any further. He chose to remain silent. But suddenly, Yvonne turned as white as a sheet: she froze and began to choke under Jean-Pierre's incredulous gaze. She barely had the strength to get up, knocking over the bottle as she went, as well as her chair. She leaned over, bent her torso at a right angle, and without hesitation plunged two fingers down her throat. Jean-Pierre, stunned by the scene and powerless to move, stared at the wine spilling onto the tablecloth, gradually forming a large crimson stain. He was roused from his torpor by Yvonne's loud burp. He saw her spit out the piece of cheese in her hand, which she immediately and casually concealed in her napkin. Then she resumed her seat as if nothing had happened. Jean-Pierre, still standing and stunned, sat down without saying a word. Yvonne poured herself a large glass of water to clear the discomfort from her throat, then, in a veiled tone that gave it a singular depth, she said:

"When I think back to the war, to all of that … to my friends, my family, it's fatal. I always swallow the wrong way!"

She poured herself another glass of water and gave Jean-Pierre a faint smile. He still couldn't get over the incident, She looked at him and said:

"There's nothing we can do about it. Most of them are dead now. You're right, I shouldn't stir things up …"

As decorum demands at the end of a meal, she placed her cutlery back on her plate in parallel.

"I'll tell you why I'm making this trip to Biarritz …"

Jean-Pierre remembered the letter: the jeopardizing of the property. Earlier, he'd been reluctant to broach the subject ….

"Are you listening, Jean-Pierre?"

He did his best to concentrate.

"I'm making this trip," she continued, "for two reasons. I'll tell you the first now, and I'll tell you the second when we get to Biarritz. Does the name *Les Ours Blancs* (The White Bears) mean anything to you?"

Jean-Pierre shook his head to say no.

"Biarritz has a tradition that goes back to 1929. Every day, whatever the season, around thirty of us, despite our advanced age, take a dip in the *Port-Vieux*. They call us the White Bears!"

Baffled, Jean-Pierre raised his eyebrows.

"It's not just old skins like me, I assure you, there are also a few youngsters! Well, I mean young, around forty, like you. I've never wanted to miss this appointment, except during the war, of course ... Would you like to join us? What do you think?"

Thoughtfully, Jean-Pierre looked towards the counter to see if the waitress was still there. But she was busy preparing for the next day's opening.

"That's it! You're not listening ..."

"Yes, I am. The White Bears ..."

Yvonne was right, he didn't listen to her anymore. In truth, he didn't believe in this bathing story; *a story of older folks who swim in all season*s; as for Yvonne's promise to reveal to him the real reason for her trip, he believed it even less. As if she had guessed his thoughts, she looked at him, and said to herself that he was not so gullible ....

She said, "Otherwise, are you not glad to take this trip with me?"

"Yes, of course," he replied absently.

"I'm going to bed. You would do well to do the same." Said Yvonne, meticulously folding her napkin and getting up.

She left the table, and after giving a final glance in the direction of Jean-Pierre, she slipped away up the stairs.

The waitress was busy behind her counter. Jean-Pierre gave her a smile, to which she did not respond. A fleeting grin on his face echoed this attempted approach which had just ended in failure. He got up and went up the stairs after saying a barely audible goodnight to the waitress.

12

Back in her room, Yvonne sat on the bed. She didn't move for a while, staring at a graphic detail on the wallpaper without seeing it. She was thinking about her life. Of what she had been; of all the lies that had taken refuge in her; of all she had not wanted to see or hear.

The buzzing, mysterious silence of the night had enveloped her in a kind of oppressive cocoon, and a multitude of murmurs and disturbing whispers were once again flowing into her mind. Suddenly, she clamped her hands over her ears. She wanted to muffle the chaotic sounds, even though she knew deep down that it wouldn't protect her from her past ….

In September 1942, at the dawn of her twentieth birthday, her father, to keep her away from Isi, forces her to sign up as a guard at the Ravensbrück camp, part of the Nazi concentration camp system reserved exclusively for women. On the day of her arrival, unaware of her surroundings, she says I'm sorry while passing a female prisoner. But as the days go by, frightened by the omnipresent barbarity in the camp, she becomes aware of the horror around her and tries to stay away. She succeeds in getting herself appointed to the uniform quartermaster's office—no doubt her father's connections had something to do with it—and, although she doesn't indulge in the massacres perpetrated daily, she is a silent witness to them. Her workplace is just a few meters from the crematorium. From her window, she can see the buildings shrouded in a thick, foul-smelling fog. She takes refuge in her work in the midst of such destruction. She chooses to see nothing of the extermination. She gets used to the horror and the smell of death ….

In 1943, she manages to escape from the camp and ends up in Paris. When her mother dies in 1944, she returns to Biarritz. At her mother's burial, as the gravediggers dig a hole in the ground, the following words come naturally to her mind:

"They're not burying her. They're hiding her …"

On her return, she sees the house emptied of its occupants and discovers her father burning compromising documents in the fireplace. This was the beginning of the debacle. Her father no longer spoke to her, and when, on Monday, March 27, shortly after 2 p.m., Allied bombers appeared from the ocean and passed over Biarritz, the warning sirens screamed. But the people of Biarritz had no idea what was about to happen; the sun was shining brightly, and the town was bustling with people. They watched without fear, happy to see the Allied squadron flying through the sky, like a foretaste of the coming liberation. But when the first bombs fell,

confusion ensued. Several neighborhoods were deci-
mated; the Port-Vieux district was devastated, thick
smoke rising into the sky, revealing ruins. In the living
room, Yvonne rushed under the piano to protect herself.
Curled up, she placed her hands over her ears. Soon after, she learned that her father had been arrested ….

Yvonne released the pressure on her ears. She
breathed a sigh of relief: it had all been so long ago …
She lay back on the bed and closed her eyes. When they
reopened, she had no memory of falling asleep. Shadows were still moving on the walls of her room. She
could see images. Cloudy at first, as if entangled in the
wallpaper patterns, they became clearer. Yvonne found
herself immersed in the film of that tragic day ….

It was Liberation Day. On the esplanade of the Biarritz casino, her clothes had been ripped off. Virtually
naked, she lay prostrate on a chair mounted on a cart
and displayed like a fairground animal. She could hear
the crowd hurling abuse at her, demanding justice and
penance.

Everyone was lining up in front of her. People spat in
her face, insulting her again and again. Vengeful
weapons clanged around her. She could feel the sharp
blade of the razor scraping across her skull. To this day,
she could feel the metal and the sort of screeching
sound it made on her scalp. Her hair fell in clumps to
her bare, dirty feet. The bristles of a painter's brush
sketched a swastika on her forehead. She still remembered the warmth between her thighs when she'd been
unable to hold back the urge to urinate—this atrocious

sensation of humiliation would sometimes resurface during the night, waking her suddenly—she could clearly hear the victorious jeers coming from all sides; the punches landed on her already swollen face. Her memory was heightened; in this room she was reliving all the exactions she had suffered decades before. She ran her tongue over the corners of her mouth, for the taste of her warm, acrid blood in her mouth was still there. She remembered how, on that fateful day, she had clung to the iodized scent coming from the ocean. It had kept her going. She had so wished to receive its spray … Finally, she recalled the exact moment when she was handed over to the mob, and her body jolted and shivered uncontrollably. On the day of her arrest, she had tried to explain the inexplicable, the reasons why she had found herself a camp guard, her exile in Paris, her return to Biarritz … But the presence of a compromising document found at the Kommandantur had sealed her fate. All these events took place just before history tipped over to the right side; the right side where she was not, where she would never be.

The explanations she gave that day failed to exonerate her. On the contrary, they made her case worse: she was tried by an FFI (Forces Françaises de l'Intérieur) tribunal for collaboration with the enemy, and narrowly escaped execution …

13

Jean-Pierre was walking nervously in his room. He was thinking about the tattoo. After pacing the length and breadth of his room, he decided to do some research on the web to find out more. He switched on his laptop, plugged in his phone, transferred the images he'd taken since the start of his journey, and activated the menu to view them. Unfortunately, a slideshow of images from his previous life popped up, distracting him from his primary objective; a couple in their summer clothes was smiling at the camera; a monument stood in the background. Jean-Pierre was proudly posing in front of his brand-new cab: his fingers, index and middle fingers spread, he was making the V of victory. Other shots had captured simple moments of their lives as a couple: their faces beaming at the lens, their bodies entwined in the waves and covered in sea spray, their friends happily raising a glass in tribute to the couple. Jean-Pierre hesitated briefly: disgusted by the picture of this lost happiness, he slipped the file into the basket, slamming the cover of his laptop. On edge, he got up to open the window, took a deep breath, then returned to his seat to view the photos of his journey with Yvonne.

Several images made him smile, but when he came across the tattoo, he stopped the slideshow dead in its tracks. He enlarged the image so as to be able to read the number. After jotting it down in the palm of his hand, he raised his head, thought for a moment and looked bleakly at the décor around him—faded wallpaper with geometric patterns, a small table wedged between two walls, curtains of a faded yellow and of dubious cleanliness, then set about researching on his computer to glean information about concentration camps and deportation.

One thing led to another, and his investigations led him to a website where he found the identity of the deportee linked to the number on Yvonne's tattoo. Additional documents described the history of the tragedy step by step.

These documents included a photo of a mansion in Biarritz, described as a place where the Germans had carried out multiple interrogations and tortures during the Occupation. Jean-Pierre's face turned pale: could this be Yvonne's house? He rushed into the bathroom and couldn't help but give back everything in his stomach. He lay on the bed for a long time, but couldn't fall asleep, so decided to go for a drive.

Huddled in his car, he was still meditating on what he had just discovered. He lifted his flask of alcohol to his mouth: it was empty. He thought about getting a drink in the inn, but the light had just gone out. Now he regretted not having drunk the wine Yvonne had ordered during the meal. He threw his flask into the glove compartment and drove off. After passing the gate, he discreetly switched off the engine and coasted down the small road that overlooked the plain. A hundred meters from the inn, he turned the ignition back on and accelerated.

14

Having parked in the parking lot of a barn converted into a nightclub with the evocative name of *La Moisson*, Jean-Pierre found himself immersed in an unlikely universe. Above the dance floor, a show of changing light colors was synchronized to the languorous rhythm of a sixties slow dance; a couple intermittently illuminated was dancing in what seemed like a desperate embrace as if it were their last dance. In the nooks and crannies of the barn, plunged into near-darkness; slumped on faded and stained candy-pink sofas placed around low tables cobbled together from plow wheels, other couples were sipping their sparkling wine. Jean-Pierre took a seat at the horseshoe-shaped counter. The barman, the owner of the place, stared at him with a knowing eye, while wiping the glass. He winked discreetly at an ageless, overly made-up hooker seated at the other end of the counter, dressed in an alluring way. She immediately approached her potential new customer with a sensuality befitting the occasion. She gazed deeply into Jean-Pierre's eyes:

"Are you on a business trip?"

Surprised, Jean-Pierre nodded no, and ordered a whisky from the boss.

"Can I have a drink?" insisted the hooker, her mouth watering.

Jean-Pierre continued to sip his drink, ignoring her but forgetting the French proverb "Qui ne dit mot consent" Who does not say a word consents. She gestured to her boss, who poured her a glass of champagne. Rolling her eyes enticingly, she raised her glass to toast. Wearily, Jean-Pierre raised his glass of whisky and emptied it in one gulp. He looked at her with a puzzled look. Drunk, he took two hesitant steps towards the exit and stumbled. The hooker caught him by the collar of his jacket.

"Oh dear! You're out of shape! Stay with us a little longer … We hardly know each other! Don't you want to talk? I'm nice, you know. I can be even nicer if you want... Come on, stay with me."

Jean-Pierre looked at her with a sullen, dead-eyed expression. The boss took advantage of the interlude to refill his glass. This was the moment she chose to get even closer. Jean-Pierre's degree of alcohol removed all restraint: with a sweeping gesture, he swung his arm over the counter and sent everything within reach flying. Before things could get out of hand, the hooker took a few steps back, looking to her boss for support. The boss waved her off and crossed to the other side of the bar to confront Jean-Pierre. He thrust the bill under his nose.

"Come on! Pay up and get out!"

Jean-Pierre's puffy eyes went from the barman to the bill without understanding. With difficulty, he extracted several crumpled bills from the bottom of his pocket, threw them disdainfully on the counter and zigzagged towards the exit.

Outside, his cell phone vibrated. He stumbled and barely caught himself on a gigantic flowerpot at the entrance. He struggled to stay on his feet. He activated the loudspeaker, grumbling under his breath. It was his ex-wife:

"Why aren't you answering?"

"Well, what do you want?"

"You've been drinking!"

After a brief silence ….

"Where are you?"

He took a few sideways steps in the deserted parking lot, looking for his cab.

"What's it to you? I'm driving an old woman to Biarritz... Are you satisfied?! I'm alone, I tell you... I don't care about your threats... You're right. Talk to the judge!"

He switched off his mobile, slipped it into his pocket, and scanned the parking lot with his remote key in all directions to locate his cab. At the far end of the parking lot, the nightlights finally flashed. He opened the door and collapsed onto the seat.

It's her fault, she left me... But Yvonne, she's a nice old lady... "Cheers Yvonne!" he said aloud, raising an imaginary glass. *I like this old lady after all... a bit crazy... but I like her.*

An idea crossed his mind: *why not get rid of the laptop?*

He stared outside, raised his arm, hesitated for a second and then gave up. He put the laptop in the glove compartment, exchanged it with the plastic bottle, which he threw away in the direction of the nightclub. The bottle bounced a few times on the ground and landed right at the hooker's feet. Jean-Pierre had a nervous laughter. The hooker was frightened and bolted towards the nightclub. Her heels clicked on the asphalt. Jean-Pierre smiled. He stretched his legs out of the cab and fell asleep.

15

Yvonne had just gotten up. She was completely naked. The folds of the sheet had retained the imprint of her body. She headed for the bathroom—a sort of corridor with an old washbasin on a column—laid out a towel to hide the mirror and began to wash herself with a glove. Her gesture, performed with ceremony, soothed the pain of her bruised body. Then she ran the glove over her tattoo again and again, as if she wanted it to fade.

As her mother used to do, she finished her toilette with a few drops of "eau de parfum" on her neck, arms and back of the neck. It wasn't quite the same scent she'd breathed on her mother's neck as a child when she'd bend down to kiss her tenderly at bedtime, but it had a woody, ambery quality that revived her memory of her mother. Those were the days when she was still allowed to visit her once a month at the hospital in Cambo-les-Bains ... [5]

---

[5]*Cambo-les-Bains. A town 15 minutes drive from Bayonne in the Labourd region of the French Basque Country. It is a spa town and was once a center for the treatment of tuberculosis.*

"Why not every day," she asked her father.

"Your mother is ill. It's not good for you to see her too often."

"But …" she replied shyly, in tears.

"There are no buts, no ifs! I want you to erase those words from your vocabulary forever!"

It was then that Yvonne sought refuge in her bedroom ….

She hated this authoritarian, despotic father. A father who had made a pact with the devil.

Back from his jaunt, Jean-Pierre staggered down the inn's corridor. He stopped briefly in front of Yvonne's room, had a doubt, and turned back. Lost, he paused for a moment in the middle of the corridor and looked up at the ceiling light. The light flickered: the bulb emitted some crackling that heralded its imminent demise. He looked again at the doors aligned through the hallway. Now he was certain that his first idea had been the right one. He retraced his steps, knocked several times and, miraculously, Yvonne's door opened. He stepped inside. The bathroom light was on, but he paid no attention to it. He lay down on the bed, folded his legs and fell asleep.

Daylight woke him. He sat up. Blinded by the light, he squinted, looking at his surroundings, unable to understand why he was in this room. A few vague memories of his previous night's outing gradually emerged: he remembered pushing away the hooker, the boss who had intervened threateningly to get him to pay up and get out of the bar, and then, nothing, a black hole.

He noticed a letter lying on the bedside table. He grabbed it and plunged it mechanically into his pocket. He continued his search for clues. In a drawer of the dresser, a photo showed a young, smiling Yvonne standing next to a German soldier. They appeared to be accomplices, posing arm in arm. This image challenged his impression of Yvonne. Hadn't she confided in him that she felt a real disgust for the occupying forces? Jean-Pierre was beginning to think that she must be keeping some unmentionable secrets to herself … He closed the drawer and searched again: under the mattress, above the wardrobe, in Yvonne's suitcase. But to no avail: he found nothing and returned to his room. He remembered seeing the letter the day before, on the freeway, during the famous episode with Mr Pantoufle. He'd picked it up on the road's emergency lane and put it in Yvonne's bag without looking at it.

He unfolded the letter; it bore the letterhead of a retirement home.

Dear Madam,

Following your letter of January 12, we would like to confirm that we are expecting you on September 28 of this year, at 9am. On the back of this letter you'll find all the information you need to know about your installation. If the date is not convenient for you, please inform us 48 hours in advance ….

Jean-Pierre raised his head. Was this Yvonne's main reason for going to Biarritz?

16

A few hours later, Jean-Pierre entered the inn's dining room. Yvonne had just finished her breakfast. His features made him look tired. He still wore on his face the guilt he had felt the day before. He had made an effort by changing his clothes and having a close shave. Discreetly, he took a seat opposite Yvonne.

"I didn't want to wake you up … she said at the outset, in a soft, conciliatory voice."

Then she added mischievously:

"Say, you snore like a lion!"

After a measured silence, she poured him a cup of coffee and leaned towards him confidentially:

"Did you find what you were looking for?"

Jean-Pierre froze ….

"You're probably wondering why I keep this photo with me?"

At that point, he assumed that Yvonne had tricked him, and deliberately left the photo on display in his room for him to find ….

"Which photo are you talking about?" he replied with a detached behavior.

"The one where I am standing next to a German soldier. Jean-Pierre, you're not innocent, I know you've found it."

Slowly, Jean-Pierre looked up at her. Of course, he remembered the photo ….

"This photo was taken in front of my father's house. It was the day before my final exam at the music conservatory. The soldier who was to accompany me the next day had insisted that I pose with him. I think he had a crush on me … in any case, I didn't have much of a choice. I didn't want to attract any suspicion. You know what I mean? In those days, you had to keep a low profile."

Feeling uncomfortable, Jean-Pierre was surprised that she was so anxious to justify herself. Why did she feel obligated to explain herself like this? And although he was burning with the desire to point this out to her, he refrained. After all, it was none of his business, and the war had been over for ages. He had other things to worry about in life than hearing her talk non-stop about that period of her life. As a child, how many times had he been told, when he didn't finish his meal, "You're not leaving the table until you've finished! If you'd been to war, you wouldn't be so picky!"

He gave in. He pretended he wanted to get some fresh air on the hotel porch and to smoke a cigarette, and slipped away.

A few puffs later, Yvonne joined him, scowling.

"Why … why did you leave like that? You didn't even take the time to have breakfast … Am I boring you with my stories?"

For a moment, Jean-Pierre considered the innocent face watching him, then looked away, taking a drag on his cigarette.

"Give me a cigarette, will you?"

With a trembling hand, weakened by the previous day's excesses, he handed her a cigarette and gave her a light. Pensive, Yvonne took a first puff without inhaling, then rejected the smoke, looking at Jean-Pierre with greedy malice:

"So this is what you call fresh air!"

Jean-Pierre looked at her, as if he didn't understand. She shrugged her shoulders with a discreet sigh.

"At my age, I don't risk much, you know … It's not one cigarette that's going to …"

Then she paused. Pensive, she took another puff, this time voluptuously, then said in a deeper voice:

"When I was still a young woman, after the war, I used to smoke a lot. I made myself a promise: if ever my existence was limited to small, insignificant pleasures … I'd end my life."

She smiled and added playfully:

"Now it's just the opposite: I'm looking for those little pleasures I've always denied myself … Today, I've decided to have fun. I want to amuse myself. Yes, I do! To enjoy myself to the fullest! I want to enjoy what little life I have left … Deep down, all these years, I've been a prisoner of my past … Now I want to live in the moment!"

"Prisoner of your past?" asked Jean-Pierre in a slightly interrogative tone.

Before answering, Yvonne took the time to take a drag on her cigarette, this time mechanically, without taking any pleasure in it.

"Yes, but today I want a clean slate! You're definitely out of step, my poor friend."

He stared at her for a long time, astonished. She looked away, nervously crushed her cigarette in an ashtray and grimaced.

"Do you mean to say that today is a bit like having a second life?" said Jean-Pierre.

"Not really, the first one didn't count …"

There was another silence. Then she added with greater gravity,

"Do you want to know why it didn't count?"

"Well … Yes."

He had said this with such an air of aloofness that she had given up trying to tell him more. Her mood was now brittle:

"Go get your things, we're leaving in five minutes. I'll pay the bill. There's no point in delaying more …"

She walked away hastily.

17

Twists of morning mist swirled around the cab. It gradually dissipated, revealing a small train station in the open countryside. The crossing bell rang. The gates lowered and the cab stopped. In the back, Yvonne waved:

"Turn around. Do it now! Do it now! I don't like it here!"

About to answer Yvonne, Jean-Pierre turned to her but gave up; a loud horn announced the imminent arrival of a freight train. With a deafening sound, it finally appeared. A roar followed by a powerful blast sent tremors through the cab's interior. Jean-Pierre waited for a relative lull before replying:

"We're in the middle of nowhere. Do you really want me to turn back'?"

Yvonne nodded with a no. They watched silently at the endless string of carriages passing in front of them. Frozen as if in a kind of dread, Yvonne began to talk, her words punctuated by the train's breezy ta dam, ta dam.

"I remember a little station just like this one. The SS dogs would throw their front paws at the deportees, growling as they forced them into the wagons. In the midst of a heavy silence … I walked along the platform, hoping to find Myriam, my pianist friend from the conservatory class. I thought: 'All these people crammed into the carriages are going to be deported to concentration camps because they're Jews! Simply because they're Jews!' I walked along the train, towards the front. I could see pairs of haggard eyes, pupils dilated with fear—staring into space, straight ahead through the skylights. Their gazes seemed frozen with amazement. I remember seeing an arm dangling between two bars of a skylight, like a disjointed puppet. All those eyes were desperately looking outside for the presence of a relative, acquaintance or friend who could have come to their aid before the train ran off to who knows where … I didn't understand it at the time. I only found out afterward. Well, afterward … Some of them threw scraps of paper through the gaps in the wagons—final farewell messages that were immediately blown away by the wind or scornfully kicked by the SS onto the tracks … The locomotive whistled for a long time. I thought it would all be over soon. The train moved off, slowly … And I stood there, on the platform, without moving. In my hand, I clutched a piece of paper I'd picked up before it fell onto the tracks."

Still filled with words and confused visions, Yvonne's eyes blurred. Two tears traced an irregular trail down her pale cheeks.

Yvonne had always decided that this episode would remain a secret; that she would never tell anyone. The opposite had just happened. Once the war was over, she had wanted to invent a new past for herself: a past without history—a past as a concert performer, a past of travel, success and encounters. A past free of war, pain and drama, a past at the side of a husband she never had … A past made up of lies, although as a concert performer, even reduced to a pittance, it did happen for a short period of time. Ironically, she had given concerts for several years under the sponsorship of the *Alliance Française*[6]. But one day, when she was giving a recital in Israel, she was panic-stricken from the start of her performance until she returned to her dressing room. Her fear was that someone in the audience would recognize her as the apprentice guard she had been for a time in the *Ravensbrück* camp. After the bows, she had rushed backstage, and had not, as was her custom, offered a final piece to the audience at the curtain call. She had shut herself away in her dressing room. She had informed the hall manager that a terrible migraine would prevent her from entertaining. On her return from tour, she had decided to give up concerts for good and devote herself to teaching. Nor did she mention what had kept her alive during the war. She had neither the strength nor the courage to do so.

---

[6]*Alliance Française*: International network of local, independent chapters promoting the French language and celebrating francophone cultures.

The last carriage of the freight train faded into the distance, revealing a strangely peaceful world of sound, made up of singing birds and the distant cough of a tractor. Yvonne's face relaxed, but when her view of the tracks was completely clear, her face froze: on the platform opposite was her friend Myriam. She was holding a piece of paper in her hand, staring at her from afar ....

18

They set off again. As they traveled on the road lined up with plane trees, Yvonne drew on her memories as if to bring back Isi's presence. She was able to imagine at will his lanky silhouette. The road was bumpy. The cab drove slowly, and Yvonne experienced once again Isis' presence. In the distance, she heard the unique tone of his violin playing the *Sarasate sonata* she had once rehearsed with him ... a moment later, his silhouette miraculously appeared on the side of the road. He stood alongside a group of gypsies, playing their sonata accompanied by the spirited pizzicatos of violins. The car passed the group of musicians. Yvonne turned to exchange a long look with him.

After about a hundred kilometers, Jean-Pierre stopped to refuel. He waited for his tank to fill up, watching from the corner of his eye as Yvonne fumbled in her bag. She caught his glance. Upset, she opened her window:

"Why are you looking at me like that? Why haven't you said anything since this morning?"

With a grumpy look on his face, Jean-Pierre put the gas pump gun in its place and closed the tank.

"What do you want me to say?" he exclaimed casually.

Upset, Yvonne didn't insist and closed the window.

Jean-Pierre, without lingering, headed for the cash register to pay.

He saw a few motorists standing and yawning at a coffee machine. Jean-Pierre purchased a few toiletries. In front of the food aisle, he hesitated for a moment, noticing bottles of alcoholic beverages. He gave up the temptation and returned to the checkout. His credit card was declined. He tried again. Another failure.

"I'll be right back"

"It's fine, it's fine. Go ahead!" responded the attendant suspiciously.

Yvonne handed him her payment card and its code. Back in the store, the attendant looked at the credit card ….

"This isn't your card!"

"So what, do you want me to pay or not?"

The attendant handed him the terminal, but as he was about to enter the code, Jean-Pierre changed his mind. He dashed to the back of the store and returned with two small bottles of whisky. After paying, he hid them in his pocket before leaving. Upon his return to the car, he found Yvonne studying a road map. She seemed to be in a cheerful mood. As he settled behind the wheel, she held the map up to his face:

"You see, we're here … You're going to head for Aurillac …"

"But that's not the right way at all!"

"No matter! I want to see the *Vallée de La Jordanne*[7] You'll see, it's a magnificent region! You'll need to take this road here …" pointing to the town of *Argentat* on the map. "I want you to discover this valley!"

She placed the map on the front seat, but Jean-Pierre paid no attention to it. He programmed his GPS with a sigh, while Yvonne watched him with skepticims. He started the engine, and they sped off down the freeway.

---

[7]*Vallée de La Jordanne*: The Jordanne river in France has its source in the Massif Central mountains, north east of the town of Aurillac. The river has carved out gorges in volcanic breccias, sinking 20 to 60 meters into a massif over 1,000 meters above sea level. The river flows through these gorges for 4 kilometers from the village of Saint-Julien to Saint-Cirgues-de-Jordanne.

19

Jean-Pierre had been cruising for some time. After a few kilometers, faithful to the itinerary suggested by Yvonne, he took the *Argentat-sur-Dordogne* exit, then, a few kilometers further on, he turned off onto a winding road overlooking the town. The narrow road rose above wild and unexpected gorges. At times, it afforded a glimpse of the distant *Monts du Cantal*[8]. From time to time, Jean-Pierre would take his eyes off the road to enjoy the scenery. At a bend in the road—on the border between the *Limousin* and *Auvergne* regions [9]—he came upon *Tours de Merle*. They stood at the center of

[8]*Monts du Cantal*, The Monts du Cantal are a mountainous massif in the mid-west of the Massif Central, France, made up of the remnants of the largest stratovolcano of Europe.

[9]*Limousin and Auvergne*: Limousin is mostly a region of hills and valleys and low mountains. The highest point in Limousin is the Mont Bessou, 977 meters, near Ussel, in the Corrèze department. Most of Auvergne belongs to the uplands of the Massif Central. Tours de Merle ('Towers of Merle') are the ruins of a castle in the commune of Saint-Geniez-ô-Merle, in the Corrèze département; a majestic medieval castle that came under attack both during the 100 Years War and then further in the Wars of Religion.

the wide and wild wooded concave shape of "cirque". Higher up, he was amazed to see an impressive group of feudal ruins on a spur bathed by a meander of the Maronne.

In the back, Yvonne was fast asleep. Jean-Pierre wanted to stretch his legs. He spotted a path on the side of the hill that led into a profusion of colorful vegetation and, after parking on the side of the road, began his walk up a steep path to the top of the hill. Halfway up, he assessed his position in relation to the cab, which was getting smaller as he climbed. When he was even higher, he saw the valley where the town of *Argentat* [10]nestled. A light, shifting mist moved with the wind and seemed to cover the town with a protective veil. Jean-Pierre was beaming. Overcome by a sense of freedom he had missed for so long, he closed his eyes, took a deep breath and enjoyed the moment. But just as he was about to descend the path, he was unpleasantly surprised to see Yvonne wandering at a distance from the cab! Panicking, he raced down the slope. As soon as he reached the road, he approached her gently and tried to reassure her. She seemed absent, looking at him as if she didn't recognize him. He helped her settle back in the car, took his place at the wheel and started off. Day-

---

[10]*Argentat*, on the banks of the famous Dordogne river, Argentat was the stronghold of the "gabarriers", known for building flat-bottomed boats they would load with trunks, planks and wooden stakes necessary for heating and construction which they would bring to the city of Bordeaux.

light was slowly fading. The sky was tormented and stormy. On the horizon appeared a flaming red glow.

Having reached the bottom of the hill, Jean-Pierre got back on the freeway. A road sign indicated that they were two hundred and fifty kilometers from Bordeaux. Lulled by the monotony of driving, he gave free rein to his fatigue and began to doze off. His eyelids would close irresistibly for a second, then his head would suddenly dip downwards. Reflexively, he would suddenly open his eyes wide. For a few kilometers, he managed to fight his tiredness, but the irrepressible urge to sleep was stronger and his eyes suddenly closed as he lost control of the cab. In semi-consciousness, he could see the landscape sliding towards him in slow motion. As if in a dream, the car swerved towards the left lane just as a lorry appeared from behind. With a screech of tires, the trucker slammed on his brakes as hard as he could, swerved to the left, and corrected his trajectory *in extremis*. He honked loudly, and Jean-Pierre finally emerged from his slumber. Aware of his erratic driving, he gave a violent jerk of the steering wheel and countersteered to avoid a possible spin. In his rear-view mirror, the lumbering mass of the lorry drew dangerously close behind him, almost touching his bumper. He then saw the truck maneuver to overtake him. When he reached the cab, the trucker leaned over to try and see him from the top of his cab. Holding the steering wheel in one hand, he insulted Jean-Pierre profusely. He then passed him at top speed, sounding his horn for a long moment.

Yvonne, who had been silent the whole time, intervened:

"Please stop! We're going to have an accident! Let me drive!"

Still in shock, Jean-Pierre didn't respond.

"I can drive, you can trust me!" she insisted.

Jean-Pierre put on his blinker and pulled into a rest area to regain his composure. He turned back to Yvonne and asked,

"Do you have your driver's license?"

Yvonne rummaged in her bag and withdrew a faded pink driver's license, crumpled and taped around the edges. It was obviously from the fifties. Jean-Pierre's eyes widened with concern,

"Are you certain you can still drive?"

"I'm still a good driver, I'm telling you …"

Jean-Pierre hesitated for a long moment, but aware of the danger he had just put them in, he didn't think it wise to doubt her ….

"All right, but if anything goes wrong, I'll drive again right away!"

Yvonne responded, saying, "I would prefer for you to sit in the back …"

Yvonne moved to the front. Jean-Pierre, ready to give up his seat, changed his mind and decided to move to the passenger seat.

"No, you'd better go to the back. You can rest there" exclaimed Yvonne.

Stubborn, Jean-Pierre didn't budge.

"I won't leave until you're in the back!" insisted Yvonne.

Wearily, he gave in and went to sit in the back. Yvonne, under Jean-Pierre's concerned gaze, set about her beginner's checklist, carefully adjusting the inside and outside mirrors, moving her seat forward until she was practically glued to the steering wheel, activating the headlights several times, and finally put her hands on steering wheel in the classical 9 and 3 steering wheel position, ready to start off. However, the car suddenly leapt forward and immediately stalled.

"Stop everything! You don't know how to drive!" screamed Jean-Pierre.

Yvonne didn't seem to have heard and responded casually: "You're clearly a stressed-out person, Jean-Pierre1"

This remark left him speechless. Meanwhile, Yvonne jerked the gearshift into neutral, put the car into first gear but forgot to disengage the clutch. The gearbox made a worrying creaking noise and, after a few jolts, Yvonne managed to get out of the parking lot by pushing first gear to the limit. Jean-Pierre, on the alert, followed her maneuvers step by step, ready to intervene just in case ....

Yvonne turned onto the freeway, disregarding the flow of traffic. A fast-moving vehicle swerved into the left-hand lane to avoid an accident. Jean-Pierre gasped.

He begged her to stop as soon as possible so he could get back behind the wheel. Instead, satisfied with her feat, Yvonne took her eyes dangerously off the road, turning her head back to answer him,

"Don't look at me! Look at the road!"

Yvonne shifted into second gear, but once again pushed the gearbox to the limit.

"Relax!" she said, as if she had everything under control. "You'd better get some rest. I assure you everything will be fine. I've never had an accident … Ever! Just make yourself comfortable. Lie down and sleep!"

In overdrive, the engine roared to within an inch of breaking.

"Get into third gear!" exclaimed Jean-Pierre.

Yvonne disengaged the clutch and, when she finally managed to shift into third gear, the gearbox emitted a high-pitched creak. Rolling his eyes, Jean-Pierre roared, saying :

"Stop right now! You're going to break the gearbox!"

"But relax! You shouldn't be worrying like this! She said in a serene tone that was particularly stressful."

Tired, Jean-Pierre gave in. He leaned back against the seat, content to watch Yvonne's every move discreetly. Yvonne confided in a reassuring voice:

"Before every concert, I'd take my car … I loved to drive. I'd drive, like this, anywhere … For miles on end. It was my yoga!"

"Get into the fourth!" ventured Jean-Pierre, in disbelief.

"But how many gears are there?" exclaimed Yvonne.

Against all odds, and despite all her clumsiness, Yvonne managed to keep the car more or less under control. Lulled by the purr of the engine, Jean-Pierre's only wish after all this stress was to close his eyes. But he remained on the alert for several kilometers. Yvonne, with a pensive, nostalgic pout, drove slowly. Much too slowly: she was driving in the middle lane, and the cars that passed her seemed to fly by like racing cars. Some drivers honked their horns, annoyed by her slowness, which oscillated between 50 and 60 km/hour. She was forced to pull over to the right-hand lane reserved for slower vehicles. Jean-Pierre, reassured at last, took a micro-nap. She took advantage of this moment to confide in him while he slept. She alternated between German and French ... without an apparent clear reason :

"I'd love to talk to you ... aber wenn ich weiß, daß Sie mir zuhören ... otherwise I couldn't express myself. Ich würde gerne mit Ihnen reden ... If I know you're listening ... werde ich es nicht schaffen."

She glanced in the rear-view mirror. Jean-Pierre's eyes were closed, but she wasn't certain whether or not he was asleep.

"If you're ever awake, just pretend you're asleep ..." she said in French. Then, cautiously, she added in German: *Sie wissen noch nichts von meinem Leben ... oder so wenig ... Erinnern Sie sich, als Sie mich gestern in der Nähe der "Place de la Nation" getroffen haben? Ich saß auf diesem öffentlichen Bank und dachte an Isi ... Es hat sechzig Jahre lang gedauert, bevor es mir gelingt, zuzugeben, dass ich ihn höchst wahrscheinlich nie wieder sehen werde! Können Sie sich das vorstellen, sechzig Jahre lang zu warten?* She repeated the same words to herself approximately in French, "You don't know anything about me yet ... Or so little! Remember when you found me yesterday near the Place de la Nation? I was thinking of Isi ... For over seventy years, I've been thinking that I'll probably never see him again. Can you imagine, sixty years hoping for his return!"

She looked in the rear-view mirror. Jean-Pierre now seemed drowsy. She chose to continue in French:

"There's something I wanted to tell you, Jean-Pierre. Isi was the only love I ever had. I've known no other. Even if I've often pretended otherwise ... Despite appearances, I'm still quite young, a sort of white goose! she said wistfully. My father didn't want me to see Isi because he was Jewish! Of course, I never listened to him. After curfew, we'd meet up at the big beach, and when he got wind of our escapades, to punish me for this love affair, as he called it, he did everything he could to keep me away."

Her voice now more solemn, she continued,

"I've been looking for Isi for months. I used my father's disreputable connections to try to find him ..."

Hesitantly, she paused and glanced at the rear-view mirror.

Jean-Pierre had just opened one eye. "Do you speak German?" he said with a long yawn.

"What's that supposed to mean?" replied Yvonne.

"I'm not supposing anything ... Never mind."

"Yes, I speak German. My father made me speak German during the war. He was of Alsatian origin. At home, he only spoke to me in Alsatian. But in the presence of his friends, I was not allowed to speak anything but German. 'Parle le *spricht Deutsch*!' he would tell me, when I spoke French or with an Alsatian dialect. This was supposedly to protect me …"

Jean-Pierre yawned again and saw a road sign for a gas station coming up. Yvonne's confidences didn't seem to interest him any more than that.

"Stop at this gas station. I need a coffee." exclaimed Jean-Pierre.

Yvonne drove towards the gas station. When the cab had stopped near the store, Jean-Pierre got out and leaned over the front door, asking: "Aren't you coming?"

She nodded for no.

"Would you like me to bring you something?"

Immersed in the limbo of her memories, she didn't answer.

20

1929, Mulhouse. Yvonne is seven years old. Her parent's comfortable apartment is walking distance from her grandfather's spinning mill factory. A Christmas tree stands in the middle of the living room. With her head raised, Yvonne watches Marie, her mother, as she arranges garlands on the branches, then delicately places the Star of David on the top. Yvonne's lungs are filled with the delicate woody fragrance of the freshly cut fir. Her mother hums *O Tannenbaum*, but she is having a hard time remembering the words of the song. As Christmas time came close, Hendricks, her mother's husband, made her learn the words of the song in German. When Hendricks is around, mother seems like a shadow in the house. She fears him. Nothing she does satisfies him. Yvonne is sad to see her mother tirelessly repeating the words:

O Tannenbaum, O Tannenbaum,
Wie treu sind deine Blätter
Du grünst nicht nur zur Sommerzeit,

Nein auch im Winter wenn es schneit.
O Tannenbaum, O Tannenbaum,
Wie treu sind deine Blätter

Yvonne helps her mom any way she can. She whispers the words in her little voice when her mom stumbles over them. But it's no use: her darling mom just can't manage it, and bursts into tears.

Yvonne doesn't understand why her mom is crying.

Yvonne's memories of her mother were distant and diffuse. Yet it was she who had passed on to her the passion for music. As a child, from her bedroom, she would hear her mother play the piano when her husband was away. In his presence, Hendricks forbade her to play. The piano was purely decorative. Hendricks was a tyrant. He imposed his law. He didn't love his wife. He'd never loved her; Yvonne was the unlikely fruit of that union. Her parents had met seven years earlier in Mulhouse, at the "Fête de la St. Jean". Their romance hadn't lasted: for Yvonne's father, it was just a one-night stand. Three months later, in September, Marie, who at the time was a pianist with the *Opéra National du Rhin*,[11] came to tell him with anguish in her stomach that she was pregnant. Hendricks wanted neither her nor the child. He dismissed her without further

---

[11]The *Opéra national du Rhin* is an opera company which performs in Alsace eastern France. It includes the Opéras in Strasbourg and Mulhouse. Since 1985 the Ballet de *l'Opéra national du Rhin*, or Ballet Du Rhin for short, a national center for choreography has been based at the Mulhouse Opera.

preamble. Marie's father, Frédéric, heard the news. He was not going to let this happen:

He spoke with anger to Hendricks, "We don't make bastards in our family! You must marry her!"

The authoritarian patriarch had made his fortune in textiles. He owed his success largely to the Germans who had helped him build his empire. He was a household name in Mulhouse. A successful man. Later, it was only natural that he put his only son into the family business. Papy regretted bitterly that Alsace was no longer under German rule. He sincerely believed that Hitler's rise to power would put Germany back on its feet. But in the summer of 1931, a young lawyer by the name of *Hans Litten*[12] had the audacity to defy Adolf Hitler by putting him on the witness stand in a trial involving Nazi activists who had stabbed two communist militants. At that point, the patriarch flew into a rage: "What! This Jew dares, in the eyes of the world, to shatter the reputation of the Nazi party!"

From that moment on, the patriarch cultivated a visceral hatred of the Jewish people, which he passed on to his son. On Christmas morning, Yvonne found a gift from her father at the foot of the tree: a moleskine notebook ….

In the men's room, Jean-Pierre checks his reflection in the mirror and grimaces: he looks like he's having a

---

[12]*Hans Litten (19 June 1903 – 5 February 1938),* German lawyer who represented opponents of the Nazis at important political trials between 1929 and 1932, defending the rights of workers during the Weimar Republic.

bad day. After a close shave, he wipes his face and heads back to the parking lot. When he opens the car door, Yvonne is surprised and flinches slightly.

"Are you sure you don't want a coffee?" smiling enigmatically.

"Notice anything?" said to her.

"Yes, you shaved."

"Is that all it does to you?"

"How do you want me to feel? We'd better get going. I've arranged the meeting in Bordeaux in an hour!"

"With your German friends?" he replies with irony.

Furious, Yvonne does not respond.

21

The cab was parked in Bordeaux along the street adjoining the *Théâtre Femina* [13]—its front wheels squarely on the sidewalk, and a good part of the rear spilling on the street. Yvonne was sitting in the driver's seat. She had a strange look on her face. Sitting beside her, Jean-Pierre was looking at her with apprehension and paralyzed him completely. She moved closer, leaned towards him, closed her eyes and offered him her lips. Tetanized by this sensual and disturbing attitude, he abruptly stepped aside. *But what does she want? What is she looking for? Has she gone mad? And what is she doing behind the wheel?* These questions raced through his mind without him being able to answer them. His heart was racing. He could hear a jerky and at first far away sound, which became louder and louder. Startled, Jean-Pierre awoke. Yvonne was not by his side. He turned his head and came face to face with a policeman who had been banging on the window for some time

---

[13]The *Théâtre Femina* exists since 1921 and is still 10 rue de Grassi in Bordeaux.

and who motioned him to roll down the window. Stunned, Jean-Pierre complied:

"Is this your cab? Did you see how you're parked?"

"Er … no … yes …"

"Have you been drinking … or using illegal substances?"

His throat dry, Jean-Pierre swallowed and nodded no.

"You're a Parisian taxi. How do you explain your presence in Bordeaux?"

"I'm driving an elderly lady to Biarritz. I'm on a long-distance drive."

"Do you have the vehicle documents?"

Jean-Pierre rummaged in the glove compartment and handed over the documents. The policeman inspected them and, finding nothing to complain about, handed them back.

"Don't just stand there. Pull into the parking lot a little way ahead on your left."

Jean-Pierre was surprised to find the keys in the ignition, thanked the policeman with an embarrassed smile, and drove off.

He soon pulled into the practically deserted parking lot. Once parked, he heard the distant sound of a piano coming from the theater. He got out and headed for the stage door. He soon entered the backstage area on the garden side, close to the stage, and discovered Yvonne's silhouette—her back was slightly curved. Her virtuoso hands glided over the keyboard of a grand concert piano. She was playing a *Schubert sonata* with unique vocality, and although her fingers, somewhat numbed by age and lack of practice, occasionally stumbled over a passage, her interpretation gave the work a unique sound, a timeless eloquence, an exactness of tone served by a delicate, subtle touch, without the shadow of pianistic artifice.

For Jean-Pierre, classical music had never meant anything. He neither understood nor appreciated it. Whether it was Schubert or some other prestigious composer he didn't know about, there was nothing that remotely linked him to this musical world. He had always considered classical music to be the exclusivity of an elite group: the "bourgeois", affluent, rich, bankers, uptown minority, politicians, high society ... However, an emotion had just arisen from this musical moment which overcame at once his prejudices and certainties; his reticence vanished all at once. Unaware of what was happening to him, or of the influence this moment would have on his future life, he listened to Yvonne without moving, almost religiously. He noticed that the room was empty, except for a man sitting in the front row. Was this a continuation of his earlier dream?

Yvonne's emotion produced by the sonata was intact. Her mind had shifted into another temporality; for a moment, she could almost see the Wehrmacht officers seated in the orchestra seats ... She finished her interpretation of the sonata with a chord that resonated for a long time, like an echo of her own story.

From the auditorium, the director applauded generously, then climbed the few steps to the stage to congratulate Yvonne. She was troubled. She felt a presence behind her back. She slowly turned around, discovered Jean-Pierre almost hidden in the shadowy backstage, and beckoned him to come closer. Stunned by the moment he'd just experienced, he stepped timidly onto the stage. Yvonne introduced him to the director, who was at a loss for words to praise Yvonne's musical interpretation. He spoke German, and although Jean-Pierre could guess the spirit of what he was saying, without understanding the exact meaning, he remained reserved. But in fact, the director was speaking Alsatian, a dialect that Yvonne mastered perfectly ….

"Frédéric, I don't think my driver understands Elsässerditsch!"

The manager looked at Jean-Pierre with an embarrassed expression, and said in French, without the slightest accent:

"I'm unforgivable! I'm sorry, it's a habit … I'm delighted to meet you! he said, extending his hand. Yvonne has told me a lot about you …"

He leaned over to add discreetly:

"It's admirable what you're doing for her. Admirable!"

Jean-Pierre was surprised. He didn't understand the reason for this compliment. Uncomfortable, he didn't want to have an explanation.

"I've got a couple of little office things to take care of," added the director. I'll meet you at the *Préfecture* [14]right after. Yvonne knew the way.

The man headed backstage, but changed his mind and retraced his steps:

"I forgot. Of course, we'll be counting on your presence at the party the Prefect is giving in honor of Mademoiselle, won't we?"

Jean-Pierre hesitated for a moment, then nodded yes in acceptance.

Back at the parking lot, Jean-Pierre noticed that the cab's right fender was dented. He immediately turned to Yvonne and exclaimed:

"What the hell happened?"

Looking devastated, he walked around the vehicle and continued his inspection.

"Nothing serious," said Yvonne mildly, "Just a little bending of the fender. You didn't even wake up! Don't worry. I'll pay for the repairs."

"Were you driving?"

"Don't you remember?"

Jean-Pierre nodded tensely and settled behind the wheel. Yvonne climbed into the back, chattering happily:

"Well, the last time we stopped" said Yvonne, slamming her car door, "you had a cup of coffee which ap-

---

[14]*Préfecture*. In France, a *préfecture* is the capital city of a "department" and by metonymy also designates the office and residence of the prefect. There are 101 departments in France, thus 101 préfectures.

parently had no effect. You insisted that I take the wheel! Don't you remember?" In doubt, and beset by various contradictory thoughts, Jean-Pierre didn't insist.

"I wish you'd talked to me about music instead of bodywork …" she responded.

Jean-Pierre turned around and leaning back, said,

"Well, my specialty is bodywork and by the way, don't keep slamming the door like that!"

With a grumpy expression, he turned away, and that was the end of the discussion.

22

When they arrived at the *Préfecture* they found themselves blocked in front of a wrought-iron gate with numerous Empire-style ornamental motifs. A policeman approached to check the invitations they didn't have. Jean-Pierre opened his window to parley, but Yvonne cut him short:

"We're expected. Tell *Monsieur le Préfet* that Mademoiselle Yvonne has arrived. He'll understand."

The policeman withdrew to consult a register. On his return, he activated the gate.

A magnificently paved courtyard surrounded by flowerbeds, brightly lit by *Belle Époque* lampposts, served as the parking lot. An employee showed them where to park. *What trap have I fallen into again!* wondered Jean-Pierre as he maneuvered to park between two gleaming limousines. He thought his cab looked very poor compared to these luxurious cars.

They went up the outdoor stairway towards the entrance of the building. The Prefect was already there, greeting them with a smile. The man, in his sixties, with his studied elegance and meticulously polished white hair, bent down to kiss Mademoiselle's hand; she made no secret of the fact that she appreciated the tribute. Jean-Pierre, decidedly uncomfortable, stood back a few steps. He was astonished by what he considered Yvonne's complacent behavior.

In harmony with this futile, frilly provincial world, one could hear coming from the prefecture the slight inflections of light music. Jean-Pierre watched as Yvonne whispered a few words in the prefect's ear. From afar, the latter stared at Jean-Pierre with a disturbing, ill-concealed insistence; the Prefect appeared falsely bewildered, almost amused, as he listened to Yvonne's whispers. Jean-Pierre realized that he was the subject of the confidence.

Annoyed, and as to put an end to this merry-go-round, Jean-Pierre climbed a few steps to introduce himself, but at that moment the prefect turned around and beckoned a butler. The butler approached, listened to the prefect's instructions with grave attention, nodded, then joined Jean-Pierre a little lower down, inviting him to follow. The prefect gently wrapped his arm around Yvonne's frail shoulders and led her into the main guest salon. Before disappearing, he addressed a distant, friendly smile towards Jean-Pierre, who remained perplexed.

23

"De Gaulle[15] stayed here, in this room, in 1968" the butler confided to Jean-Pierre, not without a sense of pride. This historical anecdote left Jean-Pierre indifferent. He contemplated the vast room. It was sparsely but tastefully furnished. Indeed, the bed in which the General was supposed to have slept, a king-size double, took up a sizable portion of the room. Curiously, the width of the bed didn't seem proportional to its length, and it gave off a strange impression of imbalance; like a kind of wide-angle vision that made the room seem smaller. An interior decorator must have been called in, as the furniture was a clever and expensive mix of styles, ranging from classic to modern with a rococo twist.

Followed step by step by the exceedingly attentive butler, Jean-Pierre entered the bathroom, which had re-

[15]*De Gaulle, Charles de Gaulle (22 November 1890 – 9 November 1970) was a French general and statesman who led the Free French Forces against Nazi Germany in World War II. He was elected President of France in 1958 until his resignation in 1969.*

tained an old-fashioned luxury with a Carrara marble floor, imposing bathtub with elaborate fittings, double washbasin from the thirties, and walls lined with a *fleur-de-lys* patterned earthenware.

Back in the bedroom, the butler insisted on showing Jean-Pierre a dressing room hidden in the woodwork and filled with a number of luxury suits and tuxedos, protected by plastic covers stamped with the Préfecture's logo. On a shelf, several pairs of luxurious shoes, most of them new and in various sizes, seemed to be waiting for a foot to slip into them.

"Monsieur le Préfet insists that you choose whatever suits you best. If you knew how many MPs and ministers forget their tuxedos, you'd be amazed … Sometimes even presidents!" added the butler with a touch of emotion. "Monsieur le préfet also invites you to join them in the guest salon as soon as possible …"

He was about to take his leave, but added: "I almost forgot … Is the room to your liking?"

"Yes, but as for the sheets, please reassure me: they've been changed since the General's visit?" replied Jean-Pierre.

The humor-challenged butler remained stoic, but unable to mask his disappointment. He discreetly stepped aside, leaving Jean-Pierre free to choose his outfit. Once alone, Jean-Pierre decided on an evening suit with tailcoat, but much too baggy for him. However, he didn't care and had no fear of ridicule, quite the contrary ….

Once fitted with a pair of out of style Jim Weston moccasins and satisfied with his new silhouette, which he discovered through the mirror, Jean-Pierre began to execute grotesque gestures of circumstance which he accompanied with odd and loud expressions of his own making:

"Ah! Oh! Oh! Mon Dieu!"

24

Transformed from head to toe, Jean-Pierre walked through a long corridor decorated with fine woodwork, down the grand staircase, through the main hall and finally into the reception rooms. He immediately found himself plunged in a stilted atmosphere, faces frozen with tight or botoxed smiles; men and women of all walks of life moving from one lounge to another. They greeted each other, congratulated each other, exchanged conventional courtesies and made faces fully adapted to the situation. For his part, Jean-Pierre, his hair in disarray—decent looking, but somewhat disheveled – clearly revealed that he really was foreign to this social sphere.

After spending some time on the outskirts of the party, observing the merriment from afar, Jean-Pierre ventured into the maze of lounges in search of Yvonne. As he passed some of the guests, several turned around in surprise; on their faces one could almost hear their questions, "Who is this handsome man? A celebrity? An actor? Doubtless, a friend of the Prefect." Their faces expressed what was not spoken in words, a sort of mundane torpor. Other guests were engaged in down to earth gossip. What were they talking about? Various rumors, political intrigues, news stories that weren't really "new", a high-ranking woman who had been the victim of adultery and who also had a lover; a local celebrity who had just admitted his "coming out"; a corrupt MP; a CAC 40[16] company boss on the verge of bankruptcy ….

A waiter presented Jean-Pierre with a tray laden with glasses of champagne. He grabbed a glass, drank it down, put it down again and immediately grabbed another. Sipping from his glass, he observed with an amused and somewhat ironic air this typical provincial French society hungry for public recognition. He came across the theatre director among the guests, who told him in passing that the closed collar of his shirt should be finished off with a bow tie. Irritated by the remark, Jean-Pierre fulminated inwardly, saying to himself, doesn't *he have anything else to do?* Jean-Pierre took the opportunity to inquire about Yvonne. But mister "I-know-everything" (*Je-sais-tout*) remained evasive. He responded with a few uninteresting anecdotes about Yvonne. In short, Jean-Pierre learned nothing he didn't already know. In any case, nothing very informative.

---

[16]*CAC 4*0. The CAC 40 is the French stock market index that tracks the 40 largest French stocks based on the Euronext Paris market capitalization.

The director concluded that Yvonne's father's supposed collaboration with the Nazis during the Second World was probably mere gossip ... And when Jean-Pierre wanted to ask him about the Biarritz house, the Director was suddenly unable to pursue the conversation, mentioning he had to welcome several people for public relations reasons, and turned around suddenly. A few steps away, the Director turned discreetly to stare at Jean-Pierre and thinking as he walked away: *Why is this troublemaker asking me all these questions? What is this annoyer doing here?*

The guests were talking about "*de tout et de rien*" ("About everything and nothing", to chat about various unrelated sort of things of no particular importance.)—but especially about nothing. In the midst of this mundane hubbub, here and there, one could hear phrases that were very much in tune with the expected topics of discussion: politics, the European market, the new poor, the excessive taxation of the wealthy. Finally, Jean-Pierre spotted Yvonne in a discussion with a few guests standing in what looked like a "boudoir" (a private and small room in a house). He was amazed by her incredible ability to adapt to this small, posh, provincial world. It was an aspect of her character he had not suspected. In fact, he was put off by the whole thing ....

Tired of all the self-indulgent mundanity, Jean-Pierre decided to go into exile on the terrace adjoining the "salons". A seemingly shy and inexperienced young man had been staring at Jean-Pierre from afar and carefully moved forward towards him. He introduced himself briefly and handed Jean-Pierre his business card, saying modestly, "I write ('*Je suis la plume*') for Mister the Prefect." Then he added in a polished tone accompanied by a slight hissing typical of the polished society of Bordeaux: "You're in communications, I believe?".

"Absolutely" responded Jean-Pierre.

"And what line of work are you in?"

"I'm a taxi!"

"Ah!" said the young man, suddenly disappointed but at the same time intrigued. "You mean you're a chauffeur?"

"If you like. But mostly taxi driver!"

To save face, the young man gave him an understanding smile, but Jean-Pierre, who had enough of this charade, decided to put an end to the conversation with a most fanciful statement:

"I was only joking. I'm not a taxi driver …"

Hanging on Jean-Pierre's lips, the young man's eyes lit up. He seemed relieved.

"The truth is, I lied to you … I'm an undertaker" quipped Jean-Pierre. "I work mainly for the government. You see, I specialize in burying political figures: ministers, MPs, sometimes even prefects … and even people like you! When the occasion arises, of course!"

Upset, the prefect's "*plume*" discontinued the conversation and twirled elsewhere. *I got you there,* thought Jean-Pierre with a smile on his face. Walking over to the drinks counter, he grabbed a bottle of champagne and left the guests to take refuge in his room, the one that had once welcomed Charles de Gaulle.

A few moments later, with a glass of champagne in one hand and a Havana cigar in the other, he was splashing around in a bubble bath. He imitated a character he'd seen in a B-movie and dipped his cigar into the foam of his bath. His phone started to vibrate. It was his ex-wife. He didn't answer. He let himself slide slowly to the bottom of the bath and, before he was completely submerged, he let out with a loud voice: "What a bunch of idiots!"

25

The next day, Yvonne and Jean-Pierre headed for Bay-onne.[17] They followed a "route départementale"[18] that stretched as far as the eye could see all the way to the Landes[19] With her handbag on her lap, Yvonne was running her fingers over an imaginary piano keyboard, recalling the score of a Bach prelude. Jean-Pierre was discreetly watching her, astonished by these strange gymnastics, and far from imagining the emotions running through her virtuoso fingers.

After a few kilometers, she asked Jean-Pierre to make a slight detour, explaining that she had an appointment with her solicitor near *Hossegor*, a Landes Village. *Not the quickest way*, thought Jean-Pierre. He was already

[17]Bayonne: South-West capital of the Basque Country on the coast of the Atlantic, rich in gourmet and festive traditions.

[18]Routes départementales : secondary roads that connect towns and cities within a department, providing access to various locations and supplementing the national road network.

[19]Landes: A department in the Nouvelle-Aquitaine region, Southwestern France, with a long coastline on the Atlantic Ocean to the west.

familiar with the supposedly "slight" detours she had indicated so many times ….

The taxi parked near a covered market, close to a town house with a notary's office sign. Yvonne was gone for a long time. When she returned, Jean-Pierre complained to her. She replied briskly: "I've got to get my affairs in order after all!"

Around midday, they stopped for lunch at the *Auberge des Dunes* between *Plouharnel* and *Saint-Pierre-Quiberon*. As soon as they arrived, Yvonne said she wanted to be alone. Not minding, Jean-Pierre took refuge in the restaurant, which was virtually empty at this time of year. He was invited to sit down at a table where two place settings had already been laid, presumably for them.

Yvonne, sitting on a wrought iron garden chair, remembered the place fondly. She had stayed here several times, years and years ago. The first time was when she was fourteen. It was shortly after her grandfather's untimely death in 1936. Her parents had recently settled in Biarritz on the Grand-father's property. The patriarch had bought the place a few years earlier, as he used to say, "to recharge his batteries". Yvonne did not fully understand what is meant by dying. No one had ever explained it to her when she accompanied her father to Mulhouse for the funeral.

The day before, they had stayed in a small hotel in *Mulhouse*'s[20] Briand district, near the canal. That evening, her father had taken her into the underbelly of the city to go around the taverns until morning. She woke up on a bench at the back of a dark room that smelt of beer and piss. Her father was slumped over a table, snoring loudly. She shook his shoulder. He scolded her,

"Why didn't you wake me up!"

With a sob in her voice, Yvonne replied that she too was asleep.

They arrived late at the grandparents' home. Yvonne and her father didn't dare enter the flat for fear of disturbing the ceremonial burial of their grandfather. In the house, no sound came from tight-lipped mouths. They had stood on the doorstep until they were invited to pay their respects to the dead man.

The patriarch's body had been placed in what had once been his study. The coffin, still open, lay on some trestles. All impression of authority had disappeared from his face. To give him a calmer appearance, his cheeks had been made up, giving him a strangely baby-ish look. With his head positioned in line with his hands, he looked like a child; his clasped hands were resting on his swollen abdomen while his head was slightly bent over his chest. His hair had been carefully

---

[20]*Mulhouse.* The city of Mulhouse is in the historical and cultural region of Alsace in Eastern France, close to the Swiss and German borders.

combed, parted in the middle, as it had been when he was alive and ready to attend mass; the marks left by the teeth of the comb were still visible in his wiry, yellowed white hair. While Yvonne's father was still meditating as he watched the body, his mother came up to him and said, scornfully and without looking at him:

"As always. You're too late!"

While two funeral directors sealed the coffin lid, Yvonne's grandmother isolated her in the dining room. She had placed a *Kouglof*[21] on the table, then sat down opposite her granddaughter. She served her a generous slice of the cake. Coming from the room next door, the screws could be heard slowly penetrating the wood of the coffin, making small creaking sounds.

Yvonne didn't like Kouglof, but she felt compelled to eat it. The brioche was dry. She quickly stuffed her mouth with the brioche while unable to swallow properly, in the process her cheeks swelling. The cake had become mush and was lingering in her mouth, producing in her mind a deep disgust for the family. Grandma looked at her tenderly and mumbled, as if in homage to her late husband:

"Eat your Kouglof … Your grandfather loved Kouglof … Eat your Kouglof …"

Yvonne had almost choked ….

---

[21]*Kouglof*, also known as *kougelhopf* or *kougelhof*, is a traditional Alsatian brioche that is made with yeast-risen, enriched dough.

Today, the terrace, built at the edge of a pine forest, seemed more intimate to Yvonne. This impression wasn't simply due to the passage of time, or to nostalgia linked to her advanced age, but Yvonne had clung to the image she remembered of the place which in the past had seemed much larger and eerie. When young, she used to get lost in the vastness of the place, which felt like the setting for a children's story. A scary story. But in truth, it hadn't really changed, despite the fact that the forest had moved slightly in and nibbled away a few meters of the terrace.

Jean-Pierre's face displayed a profound weariness that weighed down his features and aged him. Since leaving the Prefecture, he and Yvonne had ceased speaking to each other. This silence affected him and immersed him in a kind of melancholy. However, fearing any speech on his part might be unwelcome, he went along with this silent complicity as respecting a vow of silence. As Biarritz was becoming closer, Yvonne was trying to shut off a whirlwind of mental images and had chosen to withdraw into her shell.

Jean-Pierre turned his head towards the large bay window. He could see Yvonne's silhouette sitting with her back to him, slightly hunched over, which sometimes gave the impression she carried around a lot of guilt. She seemed to be meditating. But what was on her mind? The waitress placed a carafe of water on the table.

He turned towards her and thanked her with a polite smile. When his eyes turned back to the terrace, he noticed that Yvonne had moved. She was now sitting on a chair that had been placed on the sandy path that wound through the pine forest to the sea.

The wind was beginning to pick up, and grains of sand began to perform a sort of swirling choreography. With the wind, the sand looked more like small, elongated slow worms that seemed to weave between the chairs.

Yvonne felt calmer, more serene. She took a deep breath and closed her eyes. She listened to the ebb and flow of the ocean, the crashing of the waves on the shore, which she could hear from afar. A familiar music to her ears. The emotion emanating from this place hadn't weakened with time—not even after all these years, when she had strived to escape her past and sometimes to reinvent it. Had she finally come to forgive herself? Deep in her thoughts, she breathed a slight sigh of hope. For years, she had doubted. Was she responsible for her friend Myriam's deportation to Germany? For years, she had believed that fear had driven her to denounce her best friend. She learned much later that she was in no way the cause of this tragedy. But, like a tumor lodged in her conscience, the hurt was still there.

Now, a light sea breeze caressed her face. She filled her lungs with the invigorating, salty air that intoxicated her mind. She closed her eyes and listened to the subtle rustling of the pine needles and the rustling of a large greylag goose that had just taken flight. She felt better. Her memories came back to life in the semi-darkness of her closed eyelids. The paths she had wandered in, the sturdy umbrella pine trees whose branches seemed to have been sculpted by the wind, the dunes that formed a possible rampart all the way to the edge of the beach ... all this was similar to what she had felt during her last stay long ago in the Landes.

It was summer, just before the war broke out. Peace reigned as a sweet habit; it was still the time of innocence, of lightness, of carelessness and the joy of living. The year was 1939. Her youth suddenly ended when she turned 17. She was about to discover the monster her father had become ....

With her eyes still closed, she imagined her father before her as if he were still present.

26

Settled in a classic club chair, her father holds a glass of whisky in one hand, stirring it gently to make the ice clink against the sides. His dark eyes are filled with hatred. He was having a discussion with Major Heilmann about the fate he wished to reserve for the two so-called resistance fighters who had been languishing for several days in the cellar of his house, where several cells had been set up. The interrogations had yielded nothing, and her father, against the Major's advice, wanted to get it over with: he wanted a fatal outcome.

Since the arrival of German troops on the Basque coast in June 1940, the house had become, with the complicity of his father and that of the French militia, under the benevolent gaze of the Kommandantur and the Gestapo, a place of detention in Biarritz where many resistance fighters were interrogated: a sort of antechamber to the Nazi camps. That's how Yvonne had become involved in all the atrocities that took place in that house.

Yvonne shuddered briefly as the sights and sounds came back to her. When the victims in the cellar were moaning too loudly under the beatings they endured, her father would order her to sit at the piano and work on her scales, as loud as she could, the aim being to mask the agonizing moans. When the moaning subsided, she was allowed to play pieces of her own choice. Without realizing it, she was providing assistance to the Gestapo men as they sat in the garden, chatting away: about the weather, the next tide, the next day's weather forecast, the advance of German troops westwards, Hitler's war strategy ….

Her father liked to share with his *friends* such a joyful, virile, warlike mood. Sometimes, at the end of the day, this little world would treat itself to an *apéritif*, the typical pre-dinner drink so common in France. It was offered as a reward for a job well done. Then, with shirts half-open and sleeves rolled up, the torturers didn't hide: the traces of blood visible on their shirts slowly drying in the Biarritz sunset, turning from bright red to black blood.

But Yvonne rebelled. One day, she refused to be an accomplice and cover up the complaints coming from the depths of the cellar and stopped playing. The moans rose up from the cellar into the living room and could be heard as far as the edge of the garden. Her father had been alerted and had rushed in like a madman. Yvonne's rebellion was nipped in the bud: he slammed the piano lid down on her hands with a sharp, brutal gesture. This prevented her from playing in Bordeaux for the next audition. She had to wait for weeks before recovering the use of her fingers.

During her convalescence, and to the great satisfaction of the Germans, her performance was replaced by a gramophone playing Richard Wagner's Overture to Tannhäuser. A work which, for Yvonne's father, had two advantages: firstly, of course, it camouflaged the complaints coming from the depths of the villa, and secondly, it offered the torturers the immense honor of listening to and sharing their Führer's favorite music. And so, in a reverent contemplation worthy of a midnight mass, all speech ceased. They were listening religiously to Wagner's music and smiled blissfully at this pleasant side effect of war.

Yvonne, though young and distraught, decided to leave that very day and never come back. But things turned out differently.

27

Yvonne wanted to erase from her memory and forever these terrible episodes. She tried to open her eyes again, wanting to escape the past that haunted her. She looked around for something to reassure her. She clung to a ray of light : it came through the branches of a pine tree and ended its journey on the path, making the grains of sand sparkle like particles of gold. She felt soothed by the smell of pine needles roasted by the sun. The smell of sap and honey washed over her, and she thought of her mum, her dear mum, whom she had known so little.

It was Christmas Eve. Her mum was perched on a stepladder, hanging the Star of David from the top of the Christmas tree.

"Mum, that's high. Careful, Mum! You're going to fall!" Yvonne exclaimed from the terrace.

The discoveries, the new sensations that she had felt that day, were like musical themes that transcended her gaze: Éric Satie's music was the subtle movement of sand blown back by the wind and winding its way through the juniper trees. The music of Brahms passionately proclaimed the dunes that vanished into the sea, paying homage to the rows of pine trees respectfully leaning towards the dunes. Robert Schumann's melodies, with their exaggerated romanticism, captured perfectly Yvonne's perception. Then, suddenly, deeply touched by a work of Claude Debussy, one she had so loved to perform in the past. She knew so well those delicate harmonic flights, the skillful musical counterpoints and crystalline sounds. Debussy's music was now floating in space, as if weightless above her … But when she entered the restaurant where Jean-Pierre was patiently waiting, she realized that the road to greater resilience was still a long one.

28

In Biarritz, Yvonne invited Jean-Pierre to stay with her at the *Hôtel du Palais*[22], known in the past as the *Villa Eugénie*, the imperial residence of Napoleon III and Eugénie de Montijo. At first, Jean-Pierre refused, arguing that he could stay in a more modest hotel.

"At my age, comfort is no longer a luxury!" retorted Yvonne. But this argument didn't convince Jean-Pierre at all. So, to get her way, she claimed that she wanted him to be with her so that her stay in Biarritz would be as stress-free as possible.

---

[22]*Hôtel du Palais*. Hôtel du Palais is an iconic gem of Biarritz, overlooking the Atlantic Ocean. Founded in 1854, this former imperial residence of Napoleon III and Eugénie, empress of the French from her marriage to Napoleon III on 30 January 1853 until he was overthrown on 4 September 1870.

"I don't have any specific plans, other than to go to the *Baignade des Ours blancs*[23] (White Bear Swim) So why don't you enjoy the place with me?" Jean-Pierre had no choice but to accept. He was assigned a spacious room overlooking the ocean. After sitting on the edge of the bed, he gazed out at the sea for long minutes, wondering if he was dreaming.

In the evening, they dined at the Hôtel du Palais. Throughout the meal, Yvonne remained pensive ; before the waiter brought the desserts they had chosen, she stood up. She claimed to be tired and wanting to go to bed early so as to be in good shape for the famous "White Bear Swim" scheduled for the following day. Before taking her leave, she suggested Jean-Pierre take the opportunity to relax:

"Why don't you go and enjoy yourself at the casino?"

Then she made an appointment to meet him the following morning for breakfast, and slipped away. As he ate his dessert, Jean-Pierre had plenty of time to reflect and take stock of his adventure. Whatever Yvonne had been willing to tell him, didn't seem to correspond to any kind of reality, even if certain elements of her story sometimes seemed plausible ....

---

[23]*La baignade des Ours blancs.* This is the title of the French version of this novel. The adventure of Les Ours Blancs de Biarritz began in 1929 at Port-Vieux beach, when Charles Gienger gathered participants for the first Coupe de Noël, a winter swimming race. Without a second thought and braving the seasonal cold, the various competitors took to the water, earning them their nickname.

On the basis of remarks she had made, he had carried out numerous internet searches, but most of the time they had been fruitless, apart from the famous tattoo on her arm, for which her explanation had seemed suspicious at the time ....

Although he had tried many times to get her to tell him all about herself during their journey, he was now enraged at not being able to speak frankly to her. But he suspected she'd take umbrage, or snap out of it, only to change the subject. When he'd heard her speak fluent German, he'd been surprised and told her so. While taking into account the circumstances of the time, the German occupation of France, but also the many confidences and allusions she had made concerning her father and his collaboration with the enemy, the story didn't seem clear to him; even though she had told him that her father was of Alsatian origin ... He still had many other questions. Like this devious attitude that she sometimes showed towards him when he had the audacity to ask her the main reason for coming to Biarritz. Here again, she'd always come up with the same story: the "White Bear Swim", an alleged event that he found implausible and, from his point of view, rather far-fetched. Finally, during their stay in Bordeaux, he had kept a mixed memory of this mundane episode at the prefecture. The social ambiance seemed so out of step with Yvonne's personality; he had been surprised to watch her move through it with such ease. But come to think of it, *he didn't care*. Besides, *hadn't he been paid to make this trip, and paid handsomely too?* He

153

brushed all these questions aside with a wave of his hand and decided to follow Yvonne's advice: distract himself. At a brisk pace, he made his way to the Casino Municipal de Biarritz above the main beach, a stone's throw from the Palace.

29

Jean-Pierre was perched on a stool, in a room full of slot machines and back straight as an I; lodged in front of a machine for almost an hour, he was systematically losing. Hoping in vain to salvage a win, he decided to make one last attempt: he loaded the machine to its maximum bet, restarted the game by violently activating the one-armed bandit slot machine without taking his eyes off the screen for a single moment, praying that the three reels would stabilize on the same symbols. But once again, he failed. Furious at the sight of his meagre nest egg melting away, this time he decided to bet all the money he had left. His heart pounded as he awaited the machine's verdict. When two out of three reels landed on the same symbol—in this case, a gold bar—he briefly imagined he might hit the jackpot. The suspense was unbearable: his eyes darted back and forth, searching for players who could testify to his feat. The third roller hesitated for a fraction of a second on the ingot line, but as if recovering from a weakness, turned one more notch and settled on a cherry: Jean-Pierre had just lost his entire nest egg. He got up, jerking his stool to the floor.

Like a lost soul, he wandered through the maze of machines, amidst the sonic chaos of winning jingles and the inopportune exclamations of unlucky, or rarely lucky, players. Dejected, he paused briefly to observe a player who had just landed the famous sesame. The winning alarm was sounding to warn the casino staff of the jackpot. From that moment on, his irrepressible desire to make up for lost time became so pressing that his gambling addiction took away all his judgment: he feverishly rummaged through his jacket pockets in search of Yvonne's credit card and then, without a second's hesitation, rushed to the cash dispenser. He withdrew the maximum amount authorized by the card. A few minutes later, he was already on his way to another machine.

After a brief interlude of winnings that gave him the illusion of making up for lost time, he again lost all of what he had just borrowed from Yvonne. Totally despondent, he wandered around the casino lobby for a few moments, then dropped onto a sofa facing a large bay window, with a view of the wide beach and the ocean. The sun, delicately poised on the horizon, brushed against the azure of a desperately calm sea with no swell whatsoever. A few surfers sat on their boards, waiting for the right spot, the right wave, which slow in coming. Jean-Pierre, in a morose mood, muttered cynically: *So this is Biarritz: a bunch of loonies, astride their boards, waiting for the right opportunity that never comes ... Just like me, waiting for something that could have changed my life, and won't ....*

This last remark sent him back to the way he looked at himself: without any self-esteem.

30

The next morning, as agreed, Jean-Pierre waited for Yvonne in the dining room. When she didn't show up, he asked at the reception. He was told that Mademoiselle Yvonne—the Palace staff always used this title of courtesy when mentioning her—had gone to the Port-Vieux to take part in the traditional White Bear Swim. He was handed a short note from her, "Thank you for this wonderful trip" Mademoiselle wrote simply. "Thank you for being there for me ... Forgive me for all the secrets I was unable to reveal ..."

Worried about what this short missive seemed to imply, Jean-Pierre hurried off in the direction of the Port-Vieux beach—a small cove at the end of a rocky inlet near the center of Biarritz.

The swim had evidently just ended, as several elderly bathers were emerging from the water, their bodies covered in goose bumps that gave an idea of the ocean's temperature. As the beach was being emptied of the bathers and onlookers who had come to witness the event, Jean-Pierre questioned several people, endeavor-

ing to give as accurate a description of Yvonne as possible. None of them seemed to know her, or at least remember having seen her. Discouraged, he sat on the
sand and let his gaze wander. As he was caught up in
the throbbing rhythm of the waves rolling in towards
the shore, he thought he caught a glimpse of her on a
rock. She was sitting in the lotus position, facing the
sea. For a second, he thought of the image in *Barbet
Schroeder*'s film *More*, where the silhouette of actress
Mimsy Farmer appears in this position, meditating in
front of the ocean. He got up hopeful, walked to the
edge of the shore to make sure, but had to face the
facts: it wasn't Yvonne.

An old man in a bathing suit approached Jean-Pierre.
He had been watching him for a while. The man had a
ruddy face, bushy eyebrows and a natural joviality. He
spoke up:

"Someone told me you were looking for a lady, I
imagine it's that lady over there," he said, indicating
with a shake of his head the terrace of the restaurant
overlooking the cove. Jean-Pierre immediately recognized Yvonne: she was seated, gazing at the horizon,
nostalgic, silent and pensive. The old man continued:

"Every year, this lady comes to the Baignade des
Ours Blancs, but she never swims. Could she, is not
even certain. She always sits up there, always in the
same place. The truth is," said the old man, struggling
to hide his embarrassment, "our members have always
been opposed to this lady, whom everyone calls Mademoiselle, joining our Club." He added with pride, "I've

been a member since 1957, so I know my Bears, and I can tell you: she's not one of them and never will be!"

Embarrassed, the man continued in a more confidential tone:

"This lady, well … I mean … her family," he said, gesturing with his hand, "Well, during the war, when it comes to the enemy, they behaved … Well, you know what I mean!"

The old man, embarrassed by Jean-Pierre's silence, nodded a few times with an apologetic air, then left just as he had come.

Jean-Pierre climbed a few steps, took the passageway to the restaurant terrace and joined Yvonne. As soon as he was seated, she confided in him that it was on this beach that she used to go swimming with Isi. Eighty years ago! Then he was surprised to hear her talk about her father again:

"I used to go with my father to buy sheet music in Bayonne, sometimes even Saint-Jean-de-Luz … On the way, we'd sometimes stop in front of a house, or we would enter the entrance to a building. He would ask me to write down all the Jewish-sounding names written on the mailboxes. To my surprise, he told me he was prospecting to buy a house or an apartment. He insisted that I scrupulously record every detail about these families in the moleskin notebook he'd given me for Christmas. Much later, I realized that I was just a cover for him so that he wouldn't look suspicious. That's how I became his accomplice. He then passed on this information to the German authorities. He became indispensable, and ended up working for the Gestapo …"

"And what about your mother?" interjected Jean-Pierre, troubled by her words. "You never talk about her."

"My mother? She was put into a mental institution by my father. I was still young. He allowed me to visit her, under supervision, once a month. When I went to see her, she didn't speak to me. She was absent, as if her life had evaporated …"

Yvonne noticed Jean-Pierre's stunned expression and continued:

"I saw her one last time on her birthday. Her hair had turned white. That day, a nurse was helping her eat a slice of Basque cherry cake with a spoon: 'Come on, Madame Marie! A bite for … ' With her eyes in a daze, Mum opened her mouth like a baby bird, taking bite after bite without even chewing. She had spots of inflammation at the corners of her mouth that made her look dead like … I don't think she recognized me …"

There was a silence only broken by the steady crashing of the waves, resembling the haunting reminder of things past. As the waves came and went, both Yvonne and Jean-Pierre were deep in their thoughts.

Jean-Pierre inwardly replayed, once again, the film of their trip, while Yvonne's eyes held an unsettling depth. Her story seemed to be there, confined in her eyes.

The missing pieces of the puzzle are beginning to fit together, thought Jean-Pierre. Although he wanted to question her again, he gave up when he met her gaze.

Yvonne seemed to have guessed what he was thinking. She confided in him that she had written a letter intended for him; she wanted to tell him the truth because he had not judged her. She promised to give it to him when the time came.

"This trip, I wanted it … to overcome the deep guilt that has always gnawed at me and will gnaw at me until the day I die."

The moment was ill-chosen, but Jean-Pierre, no doubt to change the subject and break the uncomfortable atmosphere, gave her back her credit card, apologizing for having used it. He promised to pay her back what he had borrowed. She reassured him that she hadn't asked for it on purpose. She had the utmost contempt for this money she had inherited from her father … Then she added suddenly:

"I'd like you to drop me off in Biarritz. I've got an important appointment."

Where? Why? Wondered Jean-Pierre. It was as if the end of this adventure was inescapable. He was taken aback that he wasn't more surprised, or even saddened, that it was all coming to an end. Yvonne wanted to go somewhere and he would drive her. He would drive her, just as he had done since the beginning of their encounter. It was as simple as that. In any case, Mademoiselle—for some time Jean-Pierre had grown accustomed to calling her that—would forever remain an enigma. He now felt that something had changed radically in the relative complicity that had been established between them. Nothing would ever be the same again. One last time, Jean-Pierre would let himself be told where to go as it happened since they left Paris, carried by the atmosphere she had imposed on him anyway; carried by her unspoken words, her share of mystery, and her lies too ... *But were they really lies? Were they not a form of truth?*

31

Once in the cab, Yvonne took from her pocket a piece of paper, on which was scribbled an address to which she wished to go. He silently drove through the winding streets of Biarritz and, at her request, stopped in front of an almost ruined house with the shutters closed. He thought he recognized the house, and noticed that the entrance gate was partly smashed in. On one of the walls, a notice from the town hall warned of its imminent destruction. This looked like the spot where the photo had been taken that had troubled him so much, a photo with Yvonne posing smiling at the side of a German soldier. There was now no doubt: this was Yvonne's family home.

"This is where I lived during the war. It's also where I died" said Yvonne, as if she were sounding the death knell of her existence. Then she asked Jean-Pierre to drop her off without delay at the address she had written down.

A few moments later, Jean-Pierre pulled up beside a wrought-iron gate through which a garden could be seen. At the far end, a small building resembling a con-valescent home bore the somewhat outdated name of *Villa du Repos* (The Rest Villa). The gate opened slow-ly, and two nurses—obviously aware of Yvonne's ar-rival – walked towards her, pushing a wheelchair up the driveway. Carefully, they took charge of Mademoiselle, who let them do so with a sort of fatalism. Jean-Pierre fetched the suitcase from the trunk and handed it to the nurses. Mademoiselle looked at Jean-Pierre, opened her handbag and handed him an envelope and a set of keys. Then she took hold of his hands and enclosed them be-tween her own.

"Jean-Pierre, I'd like to ask you a favor. It's all ex-plained in the letter I've just given you. Can I count on you?" she said hopeful and watching for his approval. Jean-Pierre nodded, not really wanting to assess what was at stake in this singular mission. He leaned over to kiss her for the first and last time. Yvonne hugged him affectionately, and finally gave him a friendly peck on the cheek, as is customary with teenagers.

"Don't be angry with me for what I said earlier. I couldn't help it. The words just escaped me … Come on, don't look like that! You knew our journey would come to an end … I'm glad we got here. That's what counts, and that's what I wanted!"

She looked deep into his eyes and added:

"You've given an old lady moments of joy …"

His vision blurred by emotion, Jean-Pierre realized that he would probably never see her again. He had become attached to Mademoiselle. She nodded discreetly to the nurses, indicating that she was ready.

The trio entered the garden of the nursing home.

The gate closed on the outside *and on her life*, thought Jean-Pierre ....

As the wheelchair moved away, he took one last look at the frail figure. He was about to leave and noticed that she raised her arm, to give him, he thought, a final sign of farewell. But the gesture was not intended for him. It was addressed to an old man who was now striding towards her. When the two were very close, Yvonne stood up, and they fell into each other's arms. They remained there for a long moment, their bodies entwined, frozen like the *Lovers of Pompeii*. From a distance, Jean-Pierre noticed, but couldn't quite make out, a mark on the old man's left forearm ... *A tattoo?* he thought for a moment. Then, after squinting to be sure, he exclaimed aloud: "Isi!" He had recognized him from the portrait Yvonne had painted of him. A portrait that was faithful to the old man's silhouette. There was no doubt in his mind: it was Isi.

32

Lost in his thoughts, Jean-Pierre drives through the streets of Biarritz. He puts Yvonne's letter on the steering wheel and discovers it:

"During the war, playing the piano was all that mattered, but I've already told you that ... I didn't want to know about anything else. I didn't want to think about what was going on in this house. Yet I knew ... But I didn't want to. I felt so weak, I was scared. I'm not proud of what I was back then. When I was freed, I paid the price ... You know, the tattoo on my arm, the one you photographed—which made me so angry—well, I didn't get that tattoo made to protect myself, contrary to what you might think. I wanted it so I'd never forget. When my father died, I inherited this house, which I never wanted to own. One last thing: this tattoo is also the combination to the safe you'll find in the house. It contains archives relating to this period. I'm asking you to donate these archives to a non-profit. You'll find the address at the bottom of this letter."

With one eye on the road, Jean-Pierre reaches into the Kraft envelope and pulls out a set of keys. Moments later, he pulls up alongside the house.

"This house is going to be destroyed. It's in a sorry state, but I assure you, the electricity has never been cut off. I've never stopped paying the bills. It'll be easy for you to get in. Horrors have happened in this house. One night, when I couldn't sleep, I went downstairs to the living room. My father ordered me to go back to bed. I refused. I told him I loved Isi. That I wanted to go away with him. I called my father a coward. I told him I couldn't stand his German friends. I was going to find Isi and never come back. He screamed at me that I was worthless. That I was a slut, like my mother. That I loved a dirty Jew. That I didn't deserve to be his daughter! He shouted at me and slapped me ..."

Jean-Pierre looks at the dilapidated house. He can't help imagining the scene.

"That day, I told him what was in my heart: that I hated him and that he'd never see me again. He slapped me again and said he'd punish me. He kept his word. A few days later, I found myself in Germany. He forced me to join the Ravensbrück camp as a guard. I was ashamed that I'd never tried to save any Jews. I probably could have. Instead, I turned a blind eye. This stayed with me all my life ... When my father died, I found archives on the deportation of Jews in the region: Isi's family name

was there. I realized that my father had denounced them. You know everything else ... Well, almost, because a few weeks ago, I received a letter from Isi. He told me he'd escaped the barbarity and had taken refuge in Biarritz for his old age! I hesitated, then decided to join him ... Jean-Pierre, don't be sad," concluded Yvonne in her letter, *"I made this trip with you, and I'm glad I did. I needed help to make this difficult journey. When you read these words, I'll be at the side of the man I've loved all my life."*

Jean-Pierre noticed a postscript at the bottom of the letter:

"In the envelope you'll find the keys to my house in L'Haÿ-les-Roses [24]*My notary will contact you and explain better than I can what I've decided to do. Don't forget to turn off the light when you get there ..."*

---

[24]*L'Haÿ-les-Roses* is a small town in the southern suburbs of Paris, France. It is located 8.5 km (5.3 mi) from the center of Paris.

33

Jean-Pierre entered the property. Climbing ivy ran along the front of the house, largely obstructing the shuttered windows. After a moment's hesitation, he walked down the driveway, overgrown with tall grass and nettles. At the front door, he turned the knob, but as the door resisted, he pushed it open with his shoulder and kicked away a pile of letters blocking the opening. Daylight revealed the dust particles that swirled in space like a grayish cloud. Jean-Pierre felt around on the wall and flicked a switch. Several bulbs from a Venetian chandelier sizzled faintly, then finally illuminated part of the room.

With measured steps, he ventured into a cathedral lounge enhanced by a wooden walkway. Art Deco furniture was overturned: four broken club armchairs were giving off their straw. In the hearth of the fireplace, documents had been burned, probably at the time of the debacle; they were as if charcoal-burned, a pungent sooty odor still present. Near the fireplace, along the wall, a baby grand was covered with a layer of dust with a gritty appearance. On its lid, a few scores with pages torn out.

Jean-Pierre ventured up the spiral staircase that led to the main corridor. It was furnished with a bookcase, on which a few books seemed to have miraculously escaped looting. He heard a creak. A picture frame had cracked under his foot. He picked it up and wiped it with the back of his sleeve. It was a portrait of Yvonne, still in her teens. Her hands rested delicately on the piano keyboard, her expression luminous, her half-closed eyes transfigured by emotion. Around her, several German soldiers seemed to be listening devoutly.

At the end of the corridor, Jean-Pierre discovered the safe and entered the code. The door creaked open. On the bottom shelf, a projector was covered by a few reels of 8mm film. Just above it, a frame held a photo of a man in his forties, staring hard into the lens: his jacket bore a swastika. *Probably Yvonne's father ...* presumed Jean-Pierre. On another shelf lay a sort of register relating to the deportation of Jews, annotated and numbered in the margin with red pencil. He stuffed all these finds into a cardboard box and hurried back down to the living room. After placing the projector on the piano lid, Jean-Pierre loaded a reel. At first, the images projected on the wall were hazy and wobbly. Then the projection stabilized, and the sequences followed each other without transition:

German soldiers posed proudly for the camera ....

From a corner of the room, young Yvonne was watching them ....

174

Facing the lens, several faces were clustered in close-up, their lips articulating words.

In an alleyway of the yard, a drunken soldier, bottle of alcohol in hand, disheveled and shirtless, ran zigzagging ....

Yvonne seemed to run away from him.

In the living room, her father observed the scene, an ironic expression on his face.

On the lid of the piano, numerous empty bottles of alcohol stood next to sheet music.

Then the picture turned dark: candles flickered everywhere in the room and outside in the yard.

Now, Yvonne was accompanying the soldiers on the piano as they sang at the top of their voices, arm in arm. *Were they singing a hymn to the Führer's glory?* wondered Jean-Pierre.

Several bottles of champagne were being poured ....

An image showed Yvonne giving the Nazi salute. With two fingers resting on her upper lip to mimic Hitler's toothbrush mustache; she acted as if reviewing the soldiers, who stood at attention as she passed.

During all these candid moments, Yvonne sometimes lent herself to the game. At other times, she appeared alone, observing her surroundings with a grave expression.

Suddenly, the projection deteriorated: numerous collisions caused the film to jitter, then a stable image finally appeared ....

A bare light bulb dangled from a wire ....

A man tied to a chair slowly raised his head to face the lens.

His face was swollen.

A gloved hand entered the field and struck him in the face. His head fell back like a puppet.

The projector misfired again and jammed: the film jammed and burned on contact with the bulb. Jean-Pierre switched off the motor. The projector's beam revealed anti-Semitic graffiti on the wall—which Jean-Pierre hadn't noticed until then—alongside other inscriptions, probably older, denouncing the owners of the premises as *collabos*. Stunned by what he had just discovered, he put an end to the projection.

He drew a file from the box at random. A photo emerged. It was another portrait of Yvonne: she was dressed as a camp guard and smiling at the camera. Her father was posing proudly at her side, one hand resting affectionately on her shoulder. Jean-Pierre turned the photo over and discovered annotations on the back: Isi's name and the date on which he and his family had been deported were there, but there was no indication of their destination. Yet just below it was a list of concentration camps. Some were annotated or crossed out … During her stay at the Ravensbrück camp, *could Yvonne have been investigating discreetly to find Isi? Was her status as guardian just a facade?* wondered Jean-Pierre. *And was this list, this famous list, the fruit of her many investigations?* Disturbed by what he had just discovered and lost in so many conjectures, Jean-Pierre closed his eyes to take stock, and drifted off to sleep.

A few moments later, he felt a strange sensation of being awake without actually being awake. He blinked just long enough to adjust to the brightness, and his gaze fell on … Yvonne.

Yes, it was her! he seemed to exclaim unconsciously.

He could see her clearly. She was sitting behind the piano, but something about her physical attitude caught his eye: she was curiously frozen like a wax model, staring at him with a smile. Her hands were resting on the keyboard, and although her fingers weren't moving, the music echoed through the room. Jean-Pierre recognized it. It was the score Yvonne had played in the theater in Bordeaux, the music that had so troubled him … He wanted to get up, but something prevented him. Tired of fighting this sudden paralysis, he felt his eyelids close again. Yvonne's voice now seemed very close. Her breath caressed his hair. He recognized her perfume.

"I'm with Isi … Forever now … This is what I wanted …"

Under the stairs, the shivering ring of an old wall telephone rang insistently. Jean-Pierre got up and went to pick it up. At the other end, he heard the sound of breathing.

"Hello! Hello!" Nothing. He waited a moment, but then the call was cut out. Placing the handset back on its base, he noticed a black notebook on a wooden board.

Then he woke up. For real, this time.

He immediately got up from the armchair and went under the stairs to pick up the phone. No dial tone, the line was disconnected. As he put the handset back on its cradle, it all came back to him: earlier, on entering the room, his eye had caught sight of the famous moleskin notebook, but in his eagerness to discover the safe upstairs, he hadn't paid much attention to it.

His dream had just reminded him of its existence ….

He turned a few pages and immediately recognized Yvonne's handwriting. The notebook was also a kind of diary, in which Yvonne recorded her meetings, impressions, and the addresses of her friends. Isi's name and address figured prominently, as did the name and contact details of her friend Myriam … *All that remained was for her father to collect the information in his daughter's notebook and continue his sad work …* mused Jean-Pierre.

EPILOGUE

Deep in his thoughts, Jean-Pierre climbed back into his cab. He put the archive box on the back seat, sat behind the wheel, took one last look at the house, and drove off.

The tenderness he now felt towards Mademoiselle was mixed with a sense of shame: feeling that he'd abused her trust. Yet Mademoiselle hadn't blamed him; she hadn't even judged him. Instead, she had modestly mentioned in her letter that she was bequeathing him her house.

Jean-Pierre smiled. He remembered what Mademoiselle had told him when they'd stopped off at the inn:

"It was the kindness of people that saved me."

Wasn't Yvonne simply putting this thought into practice to help him?

A few streets further on, he came across a vehicle with a flashing beacon guiding an exceptional convoy consisting of a backhoe loader and an excavator. It occurred to him that this convoy might be destined to de-

stroy the house. Then a page would be turned for good
….

What was Yvonne doing now? Was she by Isi's side? Close to the man she'd been hoping for all her life? He would never know, and yet, for some reason, he felt good with a relaxed smile on his lips. He understood that things in his life would never be the same again. On the freeway to Bordeaux, he was still musing, *Would he find answers to Mademoiselle's story in the many archives he was taking with him?* In the meantime, one thing was certain: it was time to return to Paris and put his life in order.

About the Author

If you benefited from this book, please consider posting an online review. Thank you in advance.

After a career as a classical musician and a fifteen-year stint as an actor, appearing in theater, television, and cinema, Mathieu Ortlieb crossed paths with the producers of the renowned TV series *Strip-Tease* on TV France 3. He directed approximately twenty of the series' most iconic films.

Since then, he has dedicated himself entirely to writing. His book, titled *Mes plus belges années* (My Most Belgian Years), recounts his experiences as a director.

Additionally, he co-authored a book set during World War II, based on an unfinished, posthumous account written by his father, Jean-Jacques Ortlieb. This account recounts his war years as a young Alsatian man: *Avec les vainqueurs* (With the Winners).

Visit the author's website at
https://www.youtube.com/c/mathieuortlieb

About the Publisher

Sulis International Press publishes select fiction and nonfiction in a variety of genres under four imprints:

- Riversong Books (fiction)

- Sulis Press (general nonfiction)

- Keledei Publications (spirituality)

- Sulis Academic Press (academic works)

For more, visit the website at
https://sulisinternational.com

Subscribe to the newsletter at
https://sulisinternational.com/subscribe/

Follow on social media
https://www.facebook.com/SulisInternational
https://twitter.com/Sulis_Intl
https://www.pinterest.com/Sulis_Intl/
https://www.instagram.com/sulis_international/